BAPTISM OF BLOOD

Punishment Battalion Series Book One

Charles Whiting
writing as
K N Kostov

SAPERE
BOOKS

BAPTISM OF BLOOD

Published by Sapere Books.

24 Trafalgar Road, Ilkley, LS29 8HH

saperebooks.com

ISBN: 978-0-85495-589-3

He who fears not to speak the truth,
however bitter it may be, is strong.
It is the weak who lie!
Solzhenitsyn

BOOK ONE: *THE GULAG RATS*

'And let me remind you of this, Colonel Katukov.
You will answer for any failing of your battalion —
with your head. Dismiss!'
Secret Police Chief Beria to Colonel Katukov,
Commander of the 333 Punishment Battalion,
Moscow, November 1941.

CHAPTER 1

The full moon was ice cold. It hung at a slant in the black velvet of the winter sky. Frost glittered silver in the skeletal branches of the trees that swayed slightly in the freezing wind that blew across the steppe. All was silent, tense expectation.

The soldiers dug in on the near bank of the Volga Canal had been drinking ration vodka steadily since midnight; still they froze in their foxholes. No one could ever resign himself to that murderous cold. Already their faces were swollen with ugly red chilblains and sores and their lips were bursting with purple scabs. Starved, freezing, frightened and miserable as they were, the only thing that kept the defenders of the Volga Canal in the line was the knowledge that two hundred metres to their rear were the machine-gunners of the NKVD, the Russian Secret Police, who would not hesitate to turn their machine-guns on anyone who attempted to flee the last-ditch position; for if the Volga Canal position were breached, there would be nothing to stop the Germans from driving to Moscow itself.

A crack! A hush! On the other side of the waterway a flare hissed into the sky. Instantly everything was bathed in the red glowing eerie light.

'*Stand by, comrades... Stand by...*' The urgent command flew from foxhole to foxhole. Everywhere each waiting Red Army man pulled off his right glove and curled his stiff fingers around the triggers of his rifle, eyes narrowed anxiously for the first sight of a German.

Like a falling angel the red flare trailed to the ground. For one long moment there was a nerve-racking, absolute silence.

The defenders could hear their own hearts thumping like a crazy triphammer. In spite of the freezing cold, many of them broke out in a heavy sweat. The Fritzes must come soon. They *must!*

'*Sturmangriff!*' the harsh voice roared from the other side of the canal. A thousand voices took up the cry. All along the opposite bank, dark shapes rose and began shoving out the little assault boats.

'*Fritzes... The Fritzes are coming... Fire!*' the battalion commander bellowed, and there was no mistaking the fear in his voice, now. 'FIRE!'

The tenth attack on the village of Krasnaya Polyana that November day had commenced...

Phosphorus grenades streamed across the river, trailing white sparks behind them furiously. They exploded in a cloudburst of blazing, cream flame. In an instant the Russian side of the canal was turned into a foaming furnace of fire. Here and there a defender broke, ran screaming from his hole, a living torch that abruptly tottered, whizzed around, beating out flames with hands that were ablaze themselves, screamed and fell, consumed by that supernatural greedy fire.

Others held their positions, heads bent against the gale of glaring white flame, waiting, waiting. And then the Fritzes were coming up the bank, scrambling and wading through a morass of skinned bodies, their jackboots slipping in the jellied bloody flesh of their dead comrades. Carried away by a fervent blood rage, screaming inhumanly, their teeth bared like those of animals, their eyes wide and shining unnaturally, the defenders poured a murderous hail of fire into the field-greys.

Germans twisted in agony on the ground. Others crawled forward, dragging their pulsating grey snakes of ripped-open guts behind them. But still they kept on coming!

Now the two lines clashed. Teeth shone white in blackened oily faces, eyes gleamed dementedly as they locked together in hand-to-hand combat, slashing, gouging, hacking, chopping, slicing, tearing, choking — rifles useless now, replaced by bayonets, shovels, knives, boots, bare hands. The tenth battle for the vital position had entered its crucial phase.

In the log-covered underground bunker, lit by the flaring-hiss, glaring-white light of the petroleum lamps, the telephones jingled alarmingly; staff officers, their unshaven faces unnaturally pale, hurried back and forth; runners threw open the blackout curtains, chests heaving wildly, breath coming in leathern-lunged gasps; clerks scribbled frantic requests for help on their pads; sweating tousled radio operators tried again and again to raise units which had been long wiped out.

'Hill 120 lost, Comrade General,' the aide reported in a hushed voice.

The general dabbed his handkerchief, laced with cheap cologne, on his bald dome and stared white-eyed at the frightened captain.

'*Lost?*' he echoed stupidly, as the bunker swayed under another salvo of enemy shells like a ship at sea, caught by a sudden storm.

Now the bad news came flooding in from the whole Volga Canal line. 'Position Mayflower lost... Sunflower overrun... Easter Flower under direct 88mm fire at seventy-five metres' range... Commander, Christmas — Star blown his brains out...'

'Oh, my God,' the general whispered in ashen-faced awe, 'my whole front is disintegrating!'

Yakhrome fell. Two hours later, at two o'clock precisely, the Germans captured Kline and were starting to press hard at Dmitrov. Just before dawn Khimki fell, which meant that the Germans were now only twenty-five kilometres away from the western suburbs of Moscow itself. Only Krasnaya Polyana continued to hold out.

Feverishly staff officers worked over their large-scale maps, consuming cigarette after cigarette, trying to restore order to the shattered canal position. One held his head between his hands. Another hung over his packing-case table, his fists clenched, as if he were restraining himself from breaking down by a sheer effort of naked will. A third bared his teeth in a grimace like a man in extreme pain. And all cursed.

As the bunker rocked to and fro under the impact of the enemy shelling, the dirt tumbling from the log ceiling with every fresh shell burst, the general poured fresh cologne on his handkerchief, to cool his sweating brow, and made his final decision, his lips twitching: '*Krasnaya will be held to the last round and the last man!*'

Dawn came reluctantly, as if hesitant to illuminate that terrible lunar landscape. Wrecked tanks, trucks and cars mixed with corpses piled three deep, dead horses and severed limbs lay there, great chunks of bloody gore mingled with the silver of frozen human brains — all together formed the new line of the Volga Canal defence, from behind which the sweat-lathered, crazy-eyed Red Army men fought back, trying to stem that field-grey tide which swept across the waterway time and time again and threatened finally to swamp them for good.

In the ugly white light of the new day, the field-greys attacked yet once more, trampling over the carpet of the dead, yelling their desperate hysterical cries, following their bold young lieutenants to their deaths.

At once the ancient machine-guns on both flanks burst into angry hysterical life. Tracer zipped flatly across the canal bank from both sides, scything away the first rank. The second rank came on still, fighting their way over their dying and dead comrades, hands clawing the air as if they were climbing an invisible ladder, eyes looking pleadingly to heaven in the moment that they were struck by that deadly fire, as if they were pleading for mercy.

But there was no mercy to be granted that morning. The Russians fired belt after belt until the barrels of the ancient Maxims glowed a dull red and the gunners were forced to rip open the flies of their dirty breeches to sluice them cool with their own urine.

Closer and closer that desperate field-grey tide crept to the canal positions. Fifty metres … twenty-five metres … twenty metres… Would nothing be able to stop them now? Fifteen metres…

In his dug-out the sweating, bearded battalion commander ordered his radio operator to send out one final message. KRASNAYA STILL HOLDING OUT… FRITZES TEN METRES AWAY… EXPEDITE RELIEF… OVER AND OUT…

Then he placed the muzzle of his pistol in his mouth, brown eyes wild with despair, unshaven ashen face contorted with disgust at himself and the metallic oily taste of the pistol, and with only the slightest of hesitation crooked his finger around the trigger and pulled it in one and the same gesture. The back of his skull erupted. The gory slurry splashed across the horrified features of the radio operator; it looked as if someone had thrown a handful of red jam across his face. That single shot seemed somehow to signal the end of that last frenzied German attempt to break the canal position. One moment they were attacking fanatically, full of determination and energy; the next they were running wildly to the rear, throwing away their weapons in their crazed desire to get out of that terrible fire, tearing and fighting with each other to escape, throwing themselves into the boiling, white-water fury of the bullet-torn canal, disappearing by their scores as their equipment dragged them under or they were hit.

And then it was over and the handful of battered, begrimed defenders were staring hollow-eyed, shoulders bent, chests heaving as if they had just run a great race, at that terrible slaughter-ground, their ears still ringing with the dying echoes of that morning battle, while a kilometre away in his bunker, the general slumped in his chair, vodka bottle clutched in his nerveless fingers, seeing nothing, feeling nothing, hearing nothing save the shaken voice of his chief-of-staff dictating the careful message to Old Leather Face, which meant that he would not be sent to a concentration camp — just yet. 'KRASNAYA POLYANA HELD... EIGHTY PER CENT CASUALTIES... TROOPS EXHAUSTED... REINFORCEMENTS IMPERATIVE...'

Moscow had been saved for another day.

CHAPTER 2

Outside the great palace it was snowing and the soft, wet flakes of snow muted the stamp of the great-coated infantry, marching through Red Square to the front, thousands and thousands of them.

The dictator, sitting at the far end of the huge, dimly-lit room on his throne-like chair, did not heed the cannon-fodder heading for the slaughter of the line. Sucking his curved-bowl, old pipe, he surveyed, instead, his marshals, his dark-brown cunning eyes veiled and giving away nothing. In their turn, the be-medalled marshals, their shoulders seemingly weighed down by the new golden epaulettes that had just been reintroduced in the style of the old Tsarist Army, in which they had all once served as NCOs, stared back at the dictator uneasily, knowing full well that this conference might well decide not just whether they might lose their commands, but also their very lives.

Finally Stalin removed his pipe from beneath his thick sensual lips and stroked back his heavy black moustache. 'Comrades,' he announced with that thick Georgian accent of his, 'the situation is grave, very grave indeed. Since the Fritzes attacked us, we have lost over two million men, most of our territory in European Russia, and now the enemy stands at the gates of Moscow itself.' He said the words without emotion, without emphasis; yet there was not one soldier there at that moment who did not feel fear trace an icy finger down the small of his back at the knowledge that he, personally, might be made accountable for that terrible defeat of the Red Army.

'We are holding them, comrade,' Voroshilov, the Minister of War, said weakly.

Stalin barely hid his contempt for the moon-faced, balding Minister, an old comrade of the pre-revolutionary days, who had now let him down so badly. '*Just!*' he hissed, pointing the stem of his pipe at the Marshal, as if he were about to unleash his rage on the unfortunate officer.

'On the Moscow Front, comrade,' square-faced, burly Marshal Zhukov said hastily, trying to defend his chief, 'we are now equal in strength to the Fritzes. Our intelligence estimates they have some half a million men concentrated around the capital. We have the same number, plus four times that number of civilians employed in strengthening the Mozhaysk Line.'

All around the outspoken Commander of the Moscow Front, the other officers drew back almost fearfully, as if they did not wish to appear in Stalin's eyes to be associated with Zhukov, once the dictator unleashed his wrath upon him.

But Stalin did not seem to object to the Marshal's words. He said, 'I agree with you, Comrade Marshal. But you are overlooking the fact that the Fritzes' superiority in tanks and artillery is twofold and in aircraft almost threefold.'

Gloomily Zhukov nodded his agreement.

'That means that when we counter-attack, our infantry lacks artillery, tank and aircraft support. Of course, our attacks always fail.' Stalin made the statement without emotion, as if he never gave one moment's thought to the human lives involved in the score or so failed counter-attacks that the Red Army had launched that November. 'More importantly, the enemy's superiority in mobile resources means that he can retain the initiative all the time. He is flexible. He can switch his attacks from the left flank to the right and to the centre just when and where he pleases.'

'The centre will hold,' Zhukov, as strong-willed and as decisive as ever, maintained doggedly. 'You have my word upon it, comrade.'

'But what about our flanks, eh?' Stalin asked quickly, his cunning eyes almost disappearing in the sea of wrinkles which covered his pock-marked yellow face that gave him his nickname of "Old Leather Face" in the Red Army. 'Tell me that, comrade. Will they hold?'

'All roads to Moscow from the east are open, comrade,' the Minister of War ventured, his shoulders hunched, almost as if he expected Stalin to deal him a physical blow because of his boldness in speaking aloud. 'We expect the first rifle divisions to begin arriving from Siberia, the Far East and Kazakhstan by the first week of December. Once they are here, we will have impenetrable flanks as well as a strong centre.'

Stalin did not reply immediately. Instead he clapped his hands like an oriental pasha. Almost at once, a servant appeared from behind the silken drapes covering the door, bearing a tray, complete with bottle, saltcellar and a glass.

Deliberately, obviously enjoying making them wait, savouring his might over these most powerful men in the Red Army, Stalin poured himself a glass of the *Gorilka* vodka, sprinkled some salt on the lip of skin formed by extending his thumb and forefinger, licked it off and then tossed down the fiery spirit with an audible sigh of pleasure.

'But do you think the Fritzes will wait until we have brought up our reserves from the East?' Stalin guffawed contemptuously and answered his own question. 'Of course, they won't! By the Black Virgin of Kazan, Comrade Minister, don't you think their intelligence doesn't know what we are doing over there?'

The Minister of War's pudgy face flushed crimson and he dropped his gaze to his highly polished jackboots like a shamed schoolboy. Next to him Marshal Zhukov frowned; he knew the swine sitting on the throne-like chair at the end of the huge ornate eighteenth-century room was right. The Fritzes had their spies everywhere. They'd know as well as the *Stavka*, the Red Army's High Command, what was going on within the Red Army.

'So what do we do while we're waiting for the reserves, eh? Play with ourselves like a bored peasant boy, eh?' Stalin said coarsely. '*No!*' There was iron in his voice suddenly. 'We must out-think the Fritzes, gamble for time, hold on and hold on again somehow until those Siberians arrive.' The Soviet dictator controlled himself. 'First we must come to a decision, comrades, *where* exactly they will attack next. Secondly we must back up our decision with whatever reserves can still be scraped together. Thirdly, we must do this.' Stalin clasped his tobacco-stained fingers together as if in prayer and rolled his dark eyes around comically, staring up at the gold and blue ceiling.

The marshals tittered politely. The crisis was over. The dictator was prepared to discuss plans now without recriminations. The Minister of War gave an audible sigh of relief; his head was saved again — for the time being. Zhukov's tense look relaxed. Now, at last, they could get on with business.

Stalin nodded to the dimple-chinned Marshal and said, 'Report!' Almost as an afterthought, he added, 'please.'

'The southern flank, as you know, comrade, has been under severe attack all this month. The enemy armour was stopped earlier on at Tula by General Boldin's 50th Army. The Fritzes then left part of their forces to cover their flanks from right and left and made a dash northwards in order to come out *east* of Moscow. Their plan was obviously to link up with their forces attacking on the northern flank and thus cut off the capital from its rear supplies, reinforcements, etc. Fortunately — for us — we managed to stop them in time and they got a bloody nose there.'

Stalin nodded his understanding. From outside there came the muted singing of marching men, but there was no power or enthusiasm in the voices of the soldiers ploughing through the snow to the front; it was as if they had already realized they were heading to their death.

'On the northern flank,' Zhukov continued, 'the situation is no less critical. The enemy has reached the Moscow-Volga Canal. In the centre of that flank at Burtsevo, they are forty kilometres from Moscow, in the south at Kashira a hundred and twenty, and at the village of Krasnaya Polyana,' — even that bold soldier hesitated fearfully, as if he already guessed the degree of shock his revelation would have on his listeners — 'the Fritzes are thirty kilometres from the capital.'

'*Thirty kilometres!*' A half-dozen of the marshals echoed the words in shocked tones and Beria, the Chief of the Secret Police, bald and bespectacled, and dwarfed by the soldiers, gasped. 'But that's only one day's march from here!'

Zhukov nodded grimly and then said: 'In short, comrades, our whole front is bent into a kind of an arc, with a strong centre, and ... and two very weak flanks. The centre will hold and I think the Fritzes know it will. It is my guess — a considered one, comrade,' he looked directly at Stalin, 'that the enemy will make his main effort on one of the flanks, or perhaps both, but I think, because of his mobility and flexibility, he will limit himself to an attack on one flank, in order to achieve total superiority there.' Again Zhukov hesitated. 'The question is, *which one?*'

There was a heavy silence in the room, as the men assembled there considered that overwhelming question, knowing that any decision would be a tremendous gamble; there were only reinforcements enough available for one single flank. The wrong decision could well bring about the fall of Moscow and that might mean the end of Russia itself!

Stalin puffed his pipe steadily, revealing nothing of what might be going through his head at that moment, while behind him the ancient clock ticked away the minutes with heavy metallic inexorability.

Suddenly he asked: 'What reserves have we available, Comrade Marshal?'

'Parts of General Kuznetsov's new 1st Shock Army,' Zhukov replied promptly.

'Then have them moved up to cover Burtsevo, Kashira and Krasnaya Polyana,' Stalin ordered.

'You have made your decision?' the Minister of War gasped. 'It is to be the northern flank, then?'

Stalin looked at him contemptuously. 'Someone has to make decisions in the Kremlin, if my soldiers are afraid to do so. Yes, the Fritzes will attack in the north; at least, at first. They are closest there to success.' Zhukov ignored his chief, the red-faced minister; he thought him an incompetent fool too. 'I agree with you, Comrade Stalin. But there are simply not enough troops available in the First Shock to reinforce all points on that front. Kuznetsov's divisions are down to the strength of brigades and his brigades are reduced to the size of battalions. The First Shock might well be able to reinforce, say,

Burtsevo and Kashira, but Krasnaya Polyana would be out of the question.'

It was then that Comrade Beria, the Head of the Secret Police, made his startling suggestion.

CHAPTER 3

'She was a gypsy from the Romany Theatre. Big, fat and juicy with wonderfully athletic thighs. I thought she was going to squeeze the very life out of me! But it was a delightful experience, my dear Colonel Sarkisov. I only hope you can duplicate the experience for me tonight with that red-headed Svanetian girl you've promised me?'

'I think you can rely on me, Comrade Beria,' Sarkisov replied in those well-remembered oily tones of his. 'And this time you won't have to use drugs or the knout on her to make her willing.'

The two men laughed and Colonel Katukov's hard face hardened even more at the sound. Even in the midst of total war, Beria could not dispense with his nightly orgy. He had to have the girls he snatched off the streets of Moscow.

The man was a monster, pure and simple. Reluctantly he forced himself to raise his fist and knock on the door of the Secret Police Chief's office.

Inside the laughter died away and Beria's voice, low and accented, for like Stalin, he, too, was a Georgian, ordered 'Come!'

Colonel Katukov straightened his impressive shoulders, drew a deep breath and wondering for the umpteenth time why Beria had sent for him at such a time, turned the handle and walked in.

Beria, dressed in an immaculate western-style suit, sat behind his enormous desk, while standing at his side the handsome Armenian Sarkisov, who did his procuring for him, hastily swept the obscene pictures of naked women he had been showing his chief into his briefcase.

Katukov's face could not quite hide its look of disgust and Beria smiled softly, following the direction of his gaze, obviously amused by the reaction of the well-known NKVD's puritan to the photographs.

'That one had an arse like a black silk cushion, Colonel,' he said provocatively. 'You could sink into it up to your loins.'

Sarkisov sniggered.

Katukov clicked to attention, barrel-chest thrust out, cap with the green cross of the NKVD set rigidly under his right arm as regulations prescribed.

'Colonel Katukov, 4th NKVD District, reporting as ordered, Comrade State Defence Committee Chairman!' he barked as if he were back on the Guards' parade ground of his teens.

Beria held his balding head between his hands and groaned in that wheedling woman's voice of his, 'Please, Comrade Colonel, you really must not shout so loud. I am not deaf, you know.'

Katukov's harshly handsome face, with its cold, grey, intelligent eyes, flushed a little. 'Please accept my apologies, comrade,' he said. 'It is the official formula.'

Beria, pinched his small gold-rimmed pince-nez closer to his nose with his thin pale hand, and indicated to the tall NKVD colonel that he should stand at ease. 'You are perhaps wondering why I sent for you at such haste, Comrade,' he commenced. 'After all, you are not perhaps one of my — er — most favourite officers at the present moment, eh?'

Again Sarkisov sniggered and Katukov's flush grew deeper, but he said nothing. Many years before, as a young ensign of the Tsarist Guards with already two George Crosses to his credit before he had reached the age of eighteen, he had learnt that a good officer never made an unnecessary comment.

Beria flicked open the dossier lying in front of him on the desk next to that feared, many-thonged, leaded knout of his. 'Katukov, Pavlovich,' he muttered, 'born 28 March 1899, volunteered Imperial Guards 1916, twice wounded Galician Front, awarded three George Crosses between '16 and '18. Deserted Denikin 1919, abandoning the Whites to join the Red Army.' He looked up quizzically. 'Opportunism?'

This time the NKVD colonel flushed not with embarrassment, but with anger. 'No, Comrade, conviction!' he rapped, 'absolute genuine conviction!'

Beria smiled, unimpressed. 'How quaint,' he said in that woman's voice of his and read on. 'Joined CHEKA in 1922 and employed in anti-partisan duties in the Ukraine. Wounded twice more and awarded Red Banner and Hero of the Soviet Union.' He sniffed. 'The man is a national hero, Sarkisov.'

This time the handsome Armenian aide did not snigger. Instead he looked at Katukov, as if he were seeing him for the first time. The colonel was not a poseur, his quick brain told him that, but still there was no denying he was a man desperate for glory. The way he held his body, tilted his face so that his jaw was firm and impressive, the bold challenging look in his eyes — all indicated that the colonel wanted to be a hero. But Sarkisov, the cynic who had seen and done everything and knew everybody's price, realized, too, that Katukov would pay any price to achieve that glory and the hero status it brought with it. Men like Colonel Katukov were dangerous.

'Organized mass deportations of the Kulaks in 1930, helped to prepare the case against the Army traitors in 1938, employed in Poland in 1939 to deal with the Polack Army —' Beria broke off and looked up at the now wooden-faced Colonel.

'Ah, yes, the Polacks. There was that business of Katyn Wood, wasn't there, Katukov? A very unfortunate business.'

The Colonel looked straight ahead and said nothing, though the watching aide could see that Katyn Wood, the massacre of the Polish Officer Corps in 1940, had touched a sore point. He wondered why; he would ask Beria after Katukov had gone.

Beria dropped the dossier back on to the desk. 'Colonel,' he announced, 'I am prepared to kiss and make up.'

'I don't understand you, comrade,' Katukov stammered in bewilderment.

'Let me explain. Once you refused an express order from me and incurred my displeasure, my severe displeasure, for doing so. Now I am giving you a chance to rehabilitate yourself. The batano' (Beria used the Georgian word for "master" and Katukov guessed he must be referring to Marshal Stalin) 'has asked me to help him to find fresh troops for the Moscow front. Naturally you know as well as I do that there are no fresh troops.' He beamed up at the colonel through his pince-nez. 'So what are we going to do?'

Katukov noted that "we"; it made him even more bewildered.

'Now, my dear Katukov,' Beria continued, still beaming at him warmly, 'where is the major source of reserve manpower in the Soviet Union today, I ask you?' The question was rhetorical, for Beria answered it himself immediately. 'There is only one place to find them — the men we need. In the Gulag.'

'*The Gulag!*' Katukov exploded. 'But, comrade, the camps contain traitors, reactionaries, pimps, whoremasters, black-marketeers, murderers, perverts.' He gasped for breath, words failing him.

'Exactly, Katukov, that is why types like that *are* in the camps in the first place.'

'But one can't make soldiers out of rats like that!' the colonel said vehemently.

'Can't one?' Beria queried, seemingly amused at the hard-faced colonel's vehemence. 'In my homeland, Georgia, we say, "out of shit, princes are made." And you, my dear Katukov, are going to do exactly that. You are going to take those rats, as you call them, and make soldiers out of them, brave, fearless, elite soldiers, who will fight to the last for their Soviet Motherland.' The smile had vanished from Beria's face now and he leaned across the big desk, his eyes boring into Katukov, 'Colonel, I want you to tour the Moscow region camps and raise a full-scale battalion immediately. Promise anyone who will fight, freedom and the immediate annulment of his sentence. There are ex-officers and soldiers enough in the camps, who fought in the Revolution, against the Poles and the Japs, and who are skilled experienced fighters. You should have no trouble in putting a battalion together speedily — and I have all the infantry weapons you will need.'

'But with permission, Comrade Beria, this is madness, absolute madness!' Katukov protested desperately. 'Assuming that I can raise a battalion from those rats, what is to stop them deserting to the enemy, once they are at the front?'

'Nothing, save *you*, Katukov,' Beria replied coldly. 'Colonel Katukov, they must fear you more than they do the Fritzes. You must tolerate no weakness, no hesitation, no disobedience. The slightest infringement of military regulations must be punished severely, even by death if necessary. The battalion you raise from the Gulag must hate you, but obey you, so that the men are prepared to go to their deaths in battle rather than incur your wrath … and let me remind you of this,

Colonel Katukov. You will answer for any failing of your battalion *with your head!* Dismiss.'

Hardly aware of what he was doing, Colonel Pavlovich Katukov stamped to attention, swung his cap to his cropped blond head, saluted and marched out into a grey Moscow afternoon, with the thunder of the German guns to the west already clearly audible.

Time was running out fast. It would not be long now before the Germans attacked again. Punishment Battalion 333 would be needed at the front soon. His mind racing, Colonel Katukov, his lean jaw hard, set and determined, lengthened his stride, like a man in a great hurry. They would obey him, fight for him, and die for him, if necessary. The Gulag rats owed a debt to Mother Russia; now they would begin to pay it back. In their own blood...

CHAPTER 4

An icy wind raced across the infinite waste beyond the snowbound fir forest. It brought with it the razor-sharp frozen snow crystals, slashing the emaciated, unshaven faces of the prisoners, as they gasped and toiled at their task under the watchful eye of their guard in his fur cap and wadded, warm jacket, rifle slung carelessly over his shoulder (for what would be the usc of escaping in this frozen wilderness?) but his knout ready for action in his gloved hand.

Now there was no sound in the virgin forest save the slow rhythmic thwack of the prisoners' axes and the laboured asthmatic wheeze of the breath escaping from their terribly skinny chests after each stroke. Routinely the guard strode back and forth, his fine felt boots crunching the hard-packed snow, cracking his many-lashed whip at regular intervals, as if to encourage the prisoners to greater efforts. Another long, back-breaking, starving day at the Gulag was about over. For now the sickly yellow winter sun was sliding down beyond the horizon and already the long stark-black shadows of the night were beginning to edge across the snowy waste.

Teeth straightened his huge, heavy-muscled body up with a groan, and spat upon his calloused palms, the sweat dripping from his bushy black eyebrows in spite of the freezing cold. 'Mother of Christ,' he cursed, 'how much longer does that *schorni* expect us to work on two dried fish and a piece of black bread, eh?'

His running mate, Tinleg, twisted his metal leg around in his *valenki*, his felt boots, and looked up at the giant ex-factory worker, whose teeth had been smashed out one by one by the

NKVD when they had arrested him and replaced by the camp's dentists (all of them prisoners like themselves) by gleaming stainless steel ones, made from stolen tubing.

'What you shitting about, Teeth? As always you got the biggest *kilka*.' The *kilka* was a small dried fish.

Teeth grinned, giving his undersized, cunning-eyed companion, who had lost his right leg in the Polish campaign and had been arrested for 'military sabotage' for having stepped on the mine which had torn it while looting, the full benefit of that gleaming steel smile.

'Might is right, you little cripple,' he announced in that slow manner of his, exhibiting a fist that looked like a small ham. 'Besides I need more food than you lot of deadbeats. I'm a *real* worker.'

'Real worker,' Tinleg echoed contemptuously and raising his right haunch gave a loud wet fart. 'You and work. You've never done a real str —' His words ended in a howl of pain, as the guard's knout wrapped itself suddenly around his painfully skinny shoulders.

'Work, you son-of-a-whore!' the oily-skinned Siberian snarled, raising his whip, as if he might strike the little man again.

Teeth, his raw-boned face set abruptly, his eyes flashing angrily, half raised his axe, as if he might well cut the Siberian's skull wide open with one tremendous blow; then he lowered it again as he became aware of the noise of hooves drumming on the surface of the frozen snow.

'The *Natschalnik*,' the voice of another guard cried from across the trail at another work-party, 'the *Natschalnik* is coming!'

The guard thrust his whip hastily into his belt and unslung his rifle, crying fearfully as he did so, 'Stand to attention ... *stand to attention, will you!*'

Everywhere the weary prisoners shambled into some semblance of a line, axes balanced over their skinny shoulders, eyes set on some far horizon, as regulations prescribed, while the *Natschalnik*, Camp Commandant Proektor, cantered up on his fine white horse, accompanied (as Teeth noted from the corner of his eyes) by a tall colonel in the uniform of the NKVD, who sat on his stallion as if he had been born in the saddle.

The two riders halted in front of the ragged line and the *Natschalnik* threw back his cloak with that affected haughty manner of his and acknowledged the guards' salutes by touching his rakishly angled fur hat with his riding crop. 'Prisoners,' he announced, rising in his stirrups, as if he needed the height, 'I have brought an officer with me who has an important statement to make to you. I want you to listen carefully to all he has to say. It will be of some value to you. Comrade Colonel.'

Colonel Katukov surveyed the prisoners, shuffling their feet in the icy cold, their lips blue and their red-tipped noses running, shoulders huddled in their rags like old, old men. He wrinkled his own nose at the sight; they were not pleasant to look upon.

Standing in the front rank, Teeth did not lower his gaze as did most of the prisoners. He stared back boldly at the big officer, whose right uniform sleeve had rolled back to reveal the scars left on his wrist by sabre slashes. Now he knew where the NKVD man had learned to ride like that: undoubtedly he had fought in the Red Army cavalry against the Whites during the Civil War, as he had himself as a teenager. His eyes narrowed. What would such a man have to say of importance to them in this God-forsaken dump, he wondered.

Katukov opened his mouth, his breath fogged grey on the freezing air immediately. 'Listen, you Gulag rats,' he barked crisply, every inch the guardsman he had once been, 'once, as a young man, I was told the best way to make a speech is to stand up, speak up and shut up. That is exactly what I'm going to do now. So listen.'

Awed, even forgetting to shiver with the cold, they did just that.

'Russia needs bodies, even such poor things as yours. The Motherland is being attacked by the Fritzes on all fronts and we are suffering heavy casualties. Two million men have already been killed or taken prisoner since the war began. Now we need replacements, but there are few forthcoming — at least from the ranks of honest loyal men,' he sneered, unable to resist the dig. 'As a result, Comrade Beria is seeking volunteers from the likes of you, Gulag rats.' Katukov's voice rose. 'Step forward any man who now wishes to volunteer for service with the Red Army!'

There was an absolute silence, broken only by hoarse cawing of the frozen rooks in the snow-topped trees. No one moved.

The *Natschalnik* flushed to the roots of his dyed hair. Angrily he swept back his flowing moustache, which he pencilled darker every morning in front of his shaving mirror, and cried in that high-pitched voice of his, 'Did you not hear the Colonel? He is asking for volunteers from you scum.'

Still no one moved.

Katukov's hard gaze swept along the ranks of the prisoners until they came to rest on Teeth, who stood towering head and shoulders above his fellows. 'You… You, Gulag rat, you look as if you might once have been an honest soldier. Why don't you volunteer?'

Teeth took his time. After four years in the camps, he was afraid of nobody or nothing; he was resigned to dying in the Gulag as it was.

'Yes, Comrade Colonel,' he said slowly, 'I was an honest soldier once. I fought the Whites, the Poles and the Japanese, too, in Manchuria — and I was even promoted to the rank of sergeant-major, personally on the field of battle by the Red Eagle (Voroshilov) himself.' He paused.

Katukov waited expectantly, leaning slightly over the long steaming neck of his black stallion. 'Go on.'

'I will. And do you know what it got me, Comrade Colonel? I'll tell you. Dismissal for saying in the NCO's mess that it was perhaps wrong to purge our officers, a rotten job on the factory floor, arrest by the NKVD and my choppers systematically knocked out with a mallet by one of your green-cross friends. That's what it got me, Comrade Colonel — and you ask us to volunteer to fight for Stalin.'

Katukov was impressed by the prisoner's boldness, very impressed. Here was a fighter, he could see that all right. But he concealed his feelings behind that harshly handsome face of his. 'Do you want me to cry for you, man?' he barked. 'We've all experienced hard times since the Revolution. Mistakes were made, everyone admits that. You can't saw wood, as the peasants say, without spilling sawdust. Now your motherland needs you — and needs you urgently. The past must be forgotten.'

'Comrade Colonel?' It was the skinny runt of a man standing next to the giant who had spoken.

'Yes?'

'Patriotism is all well and good, Comrade,' Tinleg wheedled carefully, a winning look on his skinny unshaven face. 'But it don't make the goose fat. What's in it for us, if we joined you to fight for — er — Mother Russia?'

Katukov did not attempt to hide his look of contempt. This was the kind of talk he expected from the Gulag rats. 'What's in it for you scum? This. Your freedom, cancellation of sentence, and normal Red Army rations, which are equivalent to those of a heavy industrial worker.'

'Cigarettes and a vodka ration?' Tinleg asked hastily.

'Cigarettes and a vodka ration,' Katukov echoed.

'Booze and cancer-sticks — and food as well!' Tinleg yelled exuberantly, his cunning mind already racing with new plans for escaping the misery of the Gulag. 'Did you hear that? Let's volunteer!'

Caught up with sudden enthusiasm, the ragged men broke ranks and surged forward, all save a wooden-faced Teeth. But Tinleg did not give him an opportunity to back out now that there was a chance that they might not die in the hell of the Gulag after all. As the others stumbled forward, cheering and yelling at the thought of food and drink, Tinleg's metal knee thumped hard into the back of Teeth's. Automatically he staggered forward with the rest.

Five minutes later two hundred of them were swearing an oath to the Soviet Constitution on that outstretched blood-red banner that they hated so passionately. Punishment Battalion 333 had its first "volunteers".

CHAPTER 5

The Marshal squatted by himself at the far end of the bunk-lined hut. In the red-glowing gloom around the fat-bellied wood-burning stove, the old men gathered, their bearded faces hollowed out like skulls in the ruddy light. As always they were telling the old, old stories, those of the past when there were girls and food and drink. Others sat on their bunks, the legs of which rested in little bowls of water to keep off the bed-bugs, running strips of burning paper down the seams of their ragged woollen shirts, trying to kill the lice which infested them; while a few, the most fortunate ones, already snored, granted the precious boon of oblivion to the misery of the camp.

The Marshal smiled knowingly, and rolling the last of his coarse black Marhoka tobacco in a strip of newspaper torn from an old copy of *Pravda*, he fashioned and lit a cigarette. All of them, save those who were asleep, were waiting for him to make the first move, he knew that. He was a prisoner just like they were; but somehow he still remained the "Marshal", who had fought and survived Tannenberg, helped chase the Tommies out of Georgia, routed Piludski and ridden all the way to Warsaw itself, given the Japanese a bloody nose in Manchuria. Many of them were ex-officers who had been sent to the camps after the Purges and they respected the fact that he had been once the youngest Marshal in the Soviet Union before he, too, had been purged in 1938. If he volunteered, they would, too. But why should he?

The Marshal, Vladimir Boldin, pursed his bitter lips and pondered that overwhelming question. Why indeed? The Party had ruined not only his career, but also his life. For twenty years he had served it loyally and spent his blood three times for it, yet because he had once known the "Boy Marshal" in the old days, they had ordered him to report to Moscow that June and had arrested him immediately. In a way he had been fortunate: "the Boy Marshal" and seven of the other generals had been sentenced to death for high treason. Marshal Tukachevsky, Assistant Commissar for Defence, who with seven other senior officers, was charged on 12 June 1937 with the attempt to overthrow Stalin. He had "got away" with imprisonment in the Gulag. Now his wife was dead — a suicide, so the rumour had it — and his son had disappeared, probably to one of the newly formed cadet schools, designed to train the fanatically loyal "Stalin Scholars"; all because he had once served with the "Boy Marshal" twenty years before during the victorious campaign in Poland.

The Marshal sighed and rising, stared at himself in the sliver of fly-blown mirror propped against the bunk, as if to reassure himself that he still existed. A hard, masterful face, marred only by a trace of bitterness around the mouth, stared back at him. The green eyes set levelly beneath the cropped head revealed a man who knew precisely the worth of everything and everybody. Here was a soldier: a man used to command, giving orders — and having them obeyed.

He sat down again and pondered the words of the hard-faced NKVD colonel who had spoken to him in the Commandant's office that morning. In spite of the fact that the man was a policeman, he had been oddly impressive; and he, the Marshal, had felt the old thrill at the thought of violent action when Katukov, as the man had been called, had stated that this new Punishment Battalion 333 would be marching to the front immediately it had reached full strength. 'You,

Boldin, will be my second-in-command if you agree to join us,' Katukov had snapped. 'Your record as a fighting soldier is excellent and the Commandant tells me that your presence carries some weight among these Gulag traitors.'

'It is not every day that a former Marshal of the Soviet Union receives such fulsome praise,' he had answered ironically. But irony had been wasted on Colonel Katukov. He had dismissed the prisoner with, 'I expect your answer by dawn tomorrow morning. As soon as it is light I will be gone, *with* or *without* you.' And that had been that.

Now the Marshal pondered what he should do, while outside the wind howled, almost drowning the crunch of the sentries' boots on the frozen snow and the soft pad-pad of the guard dogs patrolling the outer wire.

What was he going to do?

A hundred metres away from where the Marshal squatted, engrossed in his thoughts, a weary, unshaven Colonel Katukov had his last meeting that day.

Opposite him in the empty House of Culture, stroking the half-empty bottle of pepper vodka almost as if it were a live thing, the strange-looking young man with the great horn-rimmed glasses of an intellectual hardly seemed to be listening to him at all, as Katukov explained his plans for ensuring that any disloyalty in his new battalion would be nipped in the bud. 'You see, Vulf,' he said, his lips cracked and parched from the wind and so much talking, 'undoubtedly there will be those among them who will want to seize the first opportunity of deserting either here or to the enemy. I have no illusions about that.'

Vulf thrust back a lock of lank hair, which somehow or other he had managed not to have shorn to the skull in the usual fashion of the camps, and tendered Katukov the bottle. 'Pepper vodka, they say it makes your balls grow bigger. Have a drink,' he said in his educated Moscow accent, which contrasted strongly with the crudity of his expression. □

Irritably Katukov shook his head. 'I don't drink. Now were you listening to what I just said, Vulf?'

'Yes, you asked me if I would spy for you on the other men, comrade,' Vulf said mildly, taking a deep drink from the bottle himself. 'I am to be your eyes that see and ears that listen in order that I can sing to you, comrade, like a wonderful two-legged canary.'

'Are you drunk?' Katukov snorted.

'No, I have not reached my hundred yet. It is the natural exuberance of my makeup.' Spirits were sold by the 100 grammes, hence to be drunk was to have exceeded the hundred.

The officer stared hard at the young man, who had lost his university post on account of his drinking and predicting (accurately as it turned out) to his students in Moscow that Hitler, Stalin's new ally, would one day turn on him. The NKVD had sent him to the Gulag; yet somehow he managed to have escaped the rigours of camp life, holding down the soft job of House of Culture manager. Was it because the commandant, with his absurd moustache and dyed hair, fawned upon him? Was Vulf one of those? Even in his own mind, Colonel Katukov, the NKVD's puritan, would not dare to utter the taboo word. He dismissed the unpleasant thought and said harshly, 'Well, Vulf, what's it going to be? Are you willing to work for me or not? I'm tired. I want to get to bed.'

Vulf stared at the flyblown portrait of Stalin, which was the hut's only attempt at "culture", and then outside at the stork-legged guard towers and the triple fence of barbed wire, now beginning to disappear for the day into the winter gloom.

'*Horoscho*,' he said with a sigh, 'I shall be your canary, Comrade Colonel.'

Punishment Battalion 333 had its informer.

It was about the time that Vulf sneaked into the commandant's quarters to submit himself to the impotent, fading dandy's fondling in return for a fresh bottle of pepper vodka for the last time, that the Marshal asked the ancient starosta's permission if he could talk to the rest of the hut's inmates. The bearded hut-leader, who had been in the Gulag for over ten years, agreed and now, with the *starosta* perched on his bunk, looking as if Father Time himself was presiding over their deliberations, the Marshal informed the inmates, many of whom were ex-officers like himself, what his decision was.

With the solitary candle flickering in the draught that came beneath the barred door and throwing gigantic wavering shadows on the dripping, bug-ridden walls, the Marshal explained his plan. 'Comrades,' he said, keeping his voice low so that the patrolling guards outside would not hear him, 'I shall join the NKVD bastard and become his second-in-command, the post he offered me yesterday. But,' he held up his hands, as if he expected some protest, 'it does not mean that I am selling out to that scum. It means that I — and you, too — must forget the past. Mother Russia is in danger and now our only aim must be to defeat the Fritzes. Everything else must be subordinate to that.'

'But, Comrade Marshal,' a bearded giant, with a black patch over his left eye-socket, objected, 'they're only going to use us as cannon-fodder. Those green-cross shits will throw our lives away just like that.' He clicked his thumb and forefinger together angrily.

'Don't you think I know that, Comrade Livny?' the Marshal said hastily to the one-eyed captain, who had been one of the finest intelligence officers in the Army of the Far East before his arrest. '*Horoscho*, so this Colonel Katukov can have our pimps, whoremongers and the perverts as cannon-fodder, if he wishes. Good riddance to them, though that blond chap in Hut Nine has a definitely very attractive arse on him, I must admit that.'

The listening officers laughed softly at the attempt at humour.

'But we are soldiers, experienced officers, and we *must* not let our men be sacrificed for nothing. This Colonel Katukov might think *he* is in control, but once we're at the front, comrades,' — the Marshal leaned forward, his keen gaze sweeping around their pale starved faces, and poked a thumb at his own chest — '*we* will be.'

'I see what you mean,' Livny said. 'At the front it is the fighting soldier who has the word, not those mealy-mouthed politicos.'

'Exactly.'

'But what if they put in the usual agitprop stooge, a political commissar, or even a police spy?' someone else objected. 'That kind of rat won't even be reporting to Katukov. He'll be singing directly to the Lubyanka.' The NKVD prison was infamous, and also housed Beria's office.

The Marshal curled his forefinger, as if he were pulling the trigger of a pistol. 'I've always found, comrade, that a nine-millimetre slug to the back of the right ear stops that kind of canary from singing for good.'

There was a low murmur of agreement from the others.

The Marshal held up his hands to stop it. 'Well, comrades, what is it going to be? Are you going to join me or not? And remember we are not fighting for Old Leather Face and his corrupt system — we are fighting for Mother Russia.'

'I'm with you, for one,' Livny whispered urgently.

'Me, too,' the officer who had brought up the question of the possibility of spies joined in. 'I've got a debt to pay back to the Fritzes from the Old War.' He held up his right hand. Its middle finger was missing. 'Caused me no end of grief with the girls in bed, it has, ever since 1918,' he grumbled.

There was a titter of laughter from the others and then their hands were shooting up everywhere in their eagerness to join the Marshal, their faces animated by new hope and enthusiasm.

But on the bed the old *starosta* remained unmoved, stroking his white beard slowly, as if in deep thought, staring at the younger prisoners with his faded rheumy eyes, until the Marshal could stand his gaze no longer. 'What is it, old man?' he asked. 'Why are you looking at us like that, eh?'

It seemed to take the *starosta* a long time to comprehend his question, but finally he turned his old head slowly, as if it were worked by rusty ancient springs, and croaked: 'Boldin, my friend, do not throw away your life foolishly. You must survive this war, for when you have dealt with that Fritz swine Hitler, there is another to be slaughtered in the Kremlin.' He gazed earnestly at the Marshal with his old eyes that had seen so much more of horror and of man's inhumanity to man in his ten years in the Gulag. 'I shall not live to see that glorious day, brothers, but God willing, you will.' He caught his breath and pressed a skinny claw to his side, his incredibly wrinkled face suddenly contorted with pain. 'Remember us then, brothers, remember your dead, and make that swine Stalin pay.' His voice rose and lifting his thin hand, he made the sign of the cross over their abruptly bent shaven heads.

'God bless and go with you, Gulag rats…'

BOOK TWO: *BLOODY KRASNAYA*

'Here we will fight them and here we will beat
them. Moscow will be ours by Christmas!'
General von Manteuffel, 1 December 1941.

CHAPTER 1

The little general, who in another life had been a gentleman-jockey, poised on the hillock and stared at the scene below.

Now the Russian winter was really upon them, he told himself. It had folded itself above the snowy waste like a white cloak, coating the waiting guns with thick hoar-frost and making the breath of the gunners as dense as cigar smoke every time they opened their mouths. But it had covered the debris of the last battle for the canal too, concealing the helmets, ammunition pouches, gas masks, weapons thrown away by the fleeing Ivans, hiding the stiff rigid corpses of their fallen comrades, so that now the only thing that reminded the viewer the kindly shroud of frost and snow hid a dead body was the occasional raised arm or leg, frozen solid, through which some practical joker of a signaller had threaded communication wires.

General von Manteuffel, commander of the 7th Panzer Division, tiny but tough and almost buried in his fur-collared, ankle-length greatcoat, turned his face into the icy wind racing across the frozen steppe, which seemed to lash a million crystals of razor-sharp snow into his face and could burn the unprotected skin the colour of ancient leather in minutes. He stared expectantly at the stretch of ice-covered water to his front, beyond which lay the Ivan positions. Behind him the artillery commander began to count off the seconds, 'Nine … eight … seven … three … two … one… FIRE!'

Down below, the first mortar commander echoed the order. The loader dropped his bomb down the tube. The aimer twisted his firing wheel. There was an obscene plonk. A puff of white smoke emerged from the end of the tube. Manteuffel caught a quick glimpse of the dark, fat-bellied bomb and then it was howling into the morning sky to come plummeting down an instant later.

'Dead on target!' the artillery commander roared with delight as the mortar bomb landed right on the frozen canal, the detonation ringing out with a hard resonance.

Hastily the little general focused his glasses as the next mortar fired and then the next until the artillery commander bellowed, 'Cease firing!'

Hastily he waited for the smoke to clear, ignoring the ancient Ivan machine-gun which had begun chattering on the other side of the canal like a tired woodpecker in response to the surprise bombardment.

Finally the smoke vanished, and he could see. Each bomb had hit the target. The craters in the ice were clearly apparent. Hurriedly he adjusted the binoculars, and peered through the calibrated glass, ignoring the possibility that an Ivan sniper might well be peering through a similar glass at him at that very moment, lining him up for the kill.

'Well, sir?' Captain Heinz, his aide-de-camp, asked eagerly, 'what can you see, sir?'

Manteuffel's heart leapt. 'Nothing,' he exclaimed happily, sweeping the second crater with his glasses, 'absolutely nothing. The shells haven't penetrated the ice in any of the craters.'

Heinz laughed triumphantly. 'That's a bottle of schnapps that Major Dietz of the 1st Tanks owes me. He swore last night that the ice wouldn't stand up to 81mm mortar fire.'

Manteuffel lowered his glasses and tugged the end of his long nose routinely to prevent frostbite. 'I think in all fairness, Heinz, you'd better let the major have his schnapps. Soon he and his tankers are going to need all the stimulants they can get.'

'Perhaps you're right, sir,' Heinz agreed, his happy smile vanishing at the thought of the risk Manteuffel was now prepared to take after this morning's little experiment.

Crack!

The slug howled off the branch of fir under which they were hiding, scattering snow over their shoulders. The Ivan sniper had spotted them!

Manteuffel took Heinz's arm. 'Come, young man, I think it is high time we got back to my HQ. We don't seem particularly welcome here.'

One minute later they were scampering down the deep snow of the other side of the hillock to where Manteuffel's driver was already gunning the engine of the halftrack, obviously ready for a hurried departure...

The Marshal stared up at the sniper, clad in white and tied to the tree above his head. 'Well, did you get him?' The sniper, his face crimson with cold, shook his head and grinned. 'But I gave him a damn good scare, comrade.'

The Marshal grinned back at the young soldier; obviously he took better to the freezing cold than did most of the emaciated members of the new Battalion. 'Well, that's something. But what did you make of them? They were really risking trouble standing out there. 'The tall soldier stared across the Volga Canal's frozen water at the hillock to the west where the two Fritzes had just been standing, his face puzzled.

'I can't say, Comrade Major,' the sniper replied, now busily engaged in applying the special winter grease to the lens of his telescopic rifle so that it wouldn't cloud over. 'All I know is that one of the Fritzes was a general.'

The Marshal looked up sharply. 'What did you say?'

The young sniper paused in his labour of love. 'One of 'em was a general. I could make out his stars as clear as the wart on the side of that big sergeant-major's nose over there.' He indicated Teeth, who was standing in the shelter of the snow-heavy firs, waiting for the Marshal. 'First time I've ever had a general in my sights. I'd have given a week's tobacco ration to have added him to my collection.' He slapped the butt of his rifle with a silk-gloved hand and indicated the notches for the Germans he had killed cut into the wood.

The Marshal grunted something and then, turning, walked thoughtfully back to where the big NCO was waiting, round-barrelled tommy gun cradled in his massive hands; in his grip the deadly weapon almost looked like a child's toy.

'Anything up, Comrade Major?' Teeth asked, coming out of his cover, ready to accompany the officer back to Battalion HQ.

The Marshal did not seem to have heard the question for a few moments; then he said, 'I don't know, Sergeant-major. But it does seem strange for a Fritz general to risk his neck right up here in the line.'

Teeth grinned, giving a puzzled Boldin the full benefit of that gleaming steel smile of his. 'If you ask me, comrade,' he said, 'it'd be strange for a general of *any* army to risk his neck in the line. Oh, excuse me, I forgot you —'

The Marshal waved him to be silent. 'Don't apologize, you big rogue. I know what you're thinking — generals usually die in bed.' He poked his thumb at his chest. 'And that is exactly what this particular ex-general is aiming to do. Now come on, let's see what Colonel Katukov makes of this...'

Punishment Battalion 333 had left Moscow for the Volga Canal one week before, clad in their seemingly over-large new

44

greatcoats that smelt of horse manure, their skinny, underfed frames burdened by forty kilos of equipment and weapons so that a worried Marshal had been afraid that most of them would crack up before they reached the train station. But somehow the ex-Gulag inmates had managed it, to find the station sealed off by NKVD troops armed with machine-guns and every exit barred by two-metre-high hurdles. The Marshal had swung round on a complacent Colonel Katukov and snapped, red with sudden anger at the realization why the NKVD were there. 'In three devils' name, Comrade Colonel, we have accepted your uniform and are prepared to fight in spite of the crimes committed against us! Must you make it so obvious that all we are is cannon-fodder being sent to the front to be slaughtered — like a bunch of dumb, reluctant *kulaks*?'

Katukov had shrugged and thrown away his long cigar. 'Boldin, that is exactly what you are — in my eyes. And I'm not taking any chances that half my *soldiers*,' he emphasized the word with a sneer, 'don't simply fade away into the woodwork before they board the train. I know you Gulag rats!'

But if Katukov had been suspicious of the fighting value of his new command, the haggard, unshaven young major in charge of what was left of a rifle battalion holding the sector they were relieving welcomed the newcomers as if they were a full-strength, elite Guards battalion. He ushered them into the miserable thatched peasant hunt, an *isba* that stank of unwashed bodies, boiled cabbage and black tobacco which served him as his HQ and showered the two officers with vodka and bowls of sunflower seed, his relief at being finally relieved only too obvious.

'It's not only the casualties,' he had explained, the vodka running down the stubble of his unshaven chin, while they had watched him, noting the violent trembling of his hands, mechanically cracking sunflower seeds between their teeth, 'but also the uncertainty. You know it's like the story of the two men standing in a hotel corridor, both frantically worried. The one says, "I'm a doctor and I have a patient in my room with a wooden leg, which I've taken apart and can't get back together again." And the other says, "Holy shit, that's nothing. I've got a big-bosomed redhead in my room with *both* legs apart — and I can't damn well remember my room number!"' He had laughed dutifully and a little hysterically at his own joke and added, 'That's just what I feel like out here. I know he's there, the Fritz, and I know he's going to hit us. But I don't damn well know *where* and *when* and *how* he's going to do it! That's driving me crazy.' He had drained the rest of his vodka with a greedy gulp, his hand shaking so violently that he had spilled half the liquid.

That had been a week before, and still the Fritzes had given no indication of their intention. Day after day had passed in freezing misery, with the temperature steadily dropping so that it was now zero minus twenty and the men in the line had to be ordered to check each other out every fifteen minutes to prevent their ears, noses and fingers from dying with frostbite, clusters of icicles forming at their nostrils, their helmets and eyebrows white with frost. And even when they were off-duty, huddled twenty and thirty to a hut, they could not escape that terrible cold; for the frost was like a poisonous reptile, wriggling into their uniform and blankets, biting at their extremities, creeping up arms and legs and numbing them so that within fifteen minutes most of them had been transformed into moaning, groaning blocks of ice.

The cold had become more frightening than the unseen enemy on the other side of the canal; yet a hard-faced Colonel Katukov, who the Marshal had to admit shared the freezing misery just the same as his 'Gulag rats' (as he liked to call his men), would not allow his soldiers any respite. Even when it was clear to his officers that the Fritzes were suffering from the cold just as they were, he kept all three infantry companies in the line, with only one in reserve, overriding the Marshal's protests with an iron: 'I command here. The Fritzes will come sooner or later. I want every man in the line when they do… On the day there will be no time to bring up reserves.' So the men froze and suffered, with no sign of any German activity, except, the Marshal mused grimly as he and Teeth crunched over the frozen snow back to the Battalion HQ, today.

A Fritz general in the front line. Now what exactly did that mean? But at that moment, the Marshal, famed tactician that he had been in the pre-war Red Army, had no answer to that particular question.

CHAPTER 2

'Gentlemen, there will be only cheerful faces at this conference,' Manteuffel announced, beaming around at his assembled staff officers and removing his ear-flaps.

Outside, a long weary column of Russian prisoners was shuffling by his farmhouse headquarters, herded to the rear by military policemen mounted on shaggy Siberian ponies. The little aristocrat wrinkled his nose in disgust. Even through the farmhouse's thick walls he smelt the foul odour they gave off: a combination of the biting stench he remembered from his visits to the lion house at Hagenbeck's Zoo and the filthy smell of the monkey house. He took his place at the great map which covered one wall and wished that the chain dogs, named so for the silver plates of office they wore around their necks, would hurry the Ivans past. *'Meine Herren,'* he announced, tapping the maps with the English silver-tipped riding crop he affected, 'may I have your attention, please.'

The officers turned their gaze in the direction of the aggressive little general with the cropped skull and dome-like forehead.

Manteuffel slapped the area north of Moscow, covered with a rash of red and blue crayon marks that indicated their own and enemy units, and said as if he were talking about the state of the weather, 'Here we will fight them, gentlemen, and here we will beat them.' He looked around at their faces, the usual good-humoured look gone from his keen eyes now. 'Moscow will be ours by Christmas.'

There were the grunts of protest, disbelief, even outrage, on all sides. It was just as he had expected, and as he had expected, the first protest came from his own chief-of-staff, the monocled Colonel Herber, who had still not grown used to the new style of leadership instituted by the younger panzer generals, such as himself, Rommel, Model and the rest of the rising stars. 'But, General,' he objected, 'we can hardly move the division a kilometre or more without the greatest of effort. The very oil in the motors freeze up on us, the cannons won't recoil for the same reason, and most of the men are wearing ladies' fur coats, even their red flannel knickers, in a vain effort to keep warm. Under such conditions how can we expect to get to Moscow?' Manteuffel was not impressed. 'If the Ivans can survive and fight,' he said, 'so can our soldiers. In spite of the fact that the Ivans have much superior winter clothing, our men are far better material than that.' He indicated the Russian prisoners still staggering by, most of them with their feet wrapped in rags, begging from the watching soldiers for a scrap of bread, all cringing humility, eyes anxiously on their guards and their swishing thongs.

Colonel Herber sniffed, unconvinced. 'That might well be, General,' he conceded, 'but assuming that we *could* move the division more than a couple of kilometres in the direction of the Russian capital, how are we — with the limited number of infantry available — going to cross the Volga Canal? We would need at least a regiment, perhaps even two, of infantry to make an assault crossing in order that the engineers would have sufficient cover to build a bridge for the follow-up armour.'

There was a murmur of agreement from the other staff officers of the 7th Panzer Division. Like Herber, most of them thought that Manteuffel was too brash, too pushy, too taken up by the new doctrine of attack at any price.

Manteuffel, unseen by Herber, winked cheerfully at his aide-de-camp. Heinz grinned. He knew the surprise his undersized chief was now going to spring on the stuffy divisional staff.

'Colonel Herber, I see the weather has been too cold for you to have taken your customary morning constitutional of late,' Manteuffel said.

Herber looked at the general hard, but said nothing, wondering what was coming.

'Perhaps, however, you may have noticed just how cold it has become?'

Herber looked at Manteuffel as if he had suddenly just gone mad. Of course, he had noticed how damned cold it was! If it were not for his nightly bottle of *Kognac*, he doubted whether he'd ever get a wink of sleep; it was so damned freezingly cold in his billet. 'Slightly, *Herr General*,' he remarked. 'Just very slightly.'

But irony was wasted on Manteuffel at that particular moment, as his fertile brain raced with his new plan. 'Well, then, you must have also realized that the Volga Canal, which has been holding up our troops for a month or more now, has frozen over.'

'Oh, that,' Herber said. 'Of course, General, but the Ivans are exceedingly well dug in on the other side — very tenacious defence indeed, as our casualties and those of the other attack divisions show. Attack by boat, or attack on foot, it still amounts to the same thing — a head-on assault against well-prepared defensive positions.' He shrugged easily. 'And you and I, General, veterans as we are of the Western Front in 1916, know what that means. The machine-gun always wins. Defence is trumps.'

'So you think so?' Manteuffel asked, playing the pompous opinionated chief-of-staff along.

'With all due respect, General, I don't just *think* so, I *know* so!'

'But what if those machine-guns were faced by infantry — covered by tanks?' Manteuffel persisted.

'Elephants should fly. How do we get tanks across before —' Herber broke off in mid-sentence, mouth open stupidly, and then gasped, 'But you don't mean…'

'I do!' Manteuffel cried exuberantly, his clever eyes gleaming. 'I tested the ice's strength this morning. Popped three 81mm shells down on it — at two hundred metres' range — and —'

'Go on!'

'It held!' the little general replied triumphantly. 'The damned ice held! My calculation is that if it can withstand the impact of a mortar shell at that range, it could also hold up to the weight of a Mark III tank.'

'Heaven, arse and cloudburst!' Colonel Herber chortled, his fat face suddenly flushed excitedly. 'That would be neat, exceedingly neat indeed, *Herr* General!'

'I thought you'd see the beauty of it, Colonel,' Manteuffel said, pleased with the excited looks on the faces of his staff. They were as aware as he was what a breakthrough meant; after all, they were regular officers. There'd be a corps for him, a division for Herber and promotion all round. The Führer was always very generous in such matters. 'Now then,' he continued, business-like once more, 'this is what we are going to do. First we make threatening noises on their right flank, as if we are going to attempt to outflank them there. After all, it would be, in their eyes, the logical thing to do. Then…'

Rapidly the little general sketched in his plan of attack, explaining to his attentive staff how he had already persuaded the commander of the 1st Panzer Division to his right to also launch a feint attack down there after his own attempt on the

Russian right flank had 'failed', and had been promised the support of the whole *Luftwaffe* bomber squadron for the real thing. 'It'll be the Stukas. They're slow, I know, but the Ivans have nothing to oppose them with except a few flak guns, and with those sirens of theirs howling, they'll at least put the fear of God into the Popovs, though God knows those fly boys couldn't hit the target at ten metres' range.'

The assembled staff officers, in high good humour now, laughed unnecessarily loud at the general's attempt at making fun of the *Luftwaffe*, all except the dark-haired, black-uniformed tank major at the end of the room. His handsome, intelligent face was creased in a worried frown, and when the general had finally finished his exposé and asked, in the usual formula, 'Any questions now?' he was the first to put up his hand.

'Yes, Major Dietz?'

'There is one problem, sir,' he said a little nervously, knowing that his own lack of enthusiasm for the bold plan was definitely out of place in the present assembly.

'And that is?'

'If the Popovs tumble to what we're about, and blow up the ice before we can make it with the tanks?'

'Our security is watertight, Major.' Manteuffel's confident smile faded a little as the handsome young man in the black tank corps uniform raised once again his own lingering doubts. 'There is no one, save those in this room, who know what I intend. The tank crews of the Mark IIIs won't know either until immediately before the crossing. We'll give out the story that they are being assembled at the canal bank to give the infantry additional covering fire with their 75mms as they cross.'

'But what if the Popovs spot the tin cans beforehand and tumble to what we're about, sir?' Major Deitz persisted a little desperately.

'Then, my dear young man, it will be far too late for them to plant explosives to blow up the ice,' Manteuffel answered, his response pat, for he had already considered that possibility himself. 'And what other means, do you think they would have to destroy the ice at that late stage of the game, eh?'

Dietz hung his head defeated. 'I don't know, sir,' he whispered. Manteuffel smiled, magnanimous in victory. 'There is always room for a devil's advocate in a military staff conference, Dietz,' he said easily and then, dismissing the objector, clapping his hands. The white-coated mess steward, bearing the tray of filled schnapps glasses, appeared as if he might have been listening behind the door. Hastily he started to distribute them, while Manteuffel waited, a confident smile glued to his thin lips. 'Gentlemen,' he cried, when each officer had a glass, 'let us drink a toast to victory!' He raised his own glass till it was parallel with the third button of his tunic as military regulations prescribed, arm rigid and set at a ninety-degree angle to his chest. 'Moscow by Christmas,' he bellowed. '*Prosit!*'

'Moscow by Christmas! *Prosit, Herr General!*' That coarse, confident shout filled the whole room and then glass after glass shattered against the walls, as the triumphant officers flung them against the stone with all their strength. Victory would be theirs!

CHAPTER 3

'Comrade Colonel... Comrade Colonel, wake up, please... Alarm ... *alarm*...'

At last the radio operator's frantic cries penetrated the thick black cloud of sleep. Katukov, stretched out on top of the great tiled oven that occupied one whole wall of the peasant hut, sat up, his ears already taking in the rumble of artillery to the north, to stare at the young operator's wide-eyed ashen face. 'What is it?... What damned time is it?' he asked, licking his parched lips.

'Zero five hundred hours, Comrade Colonel.'

'Two hours to dawn. And?'

'The 50th Shock Army have just radioed that they are being attacked up north and —'

The crash of fresh guns to the south drowned the rest of his words, but now Katukov needed no further explanations; the fresh gunfire told him everything. His neighbour to the south was beginning to be attacked too. The Fritzes were starting an all-out attack.

Hastily, he swung himself off the warm oven. Grabbing his boots and greatcoat, he rushed out into the freezing night. His second-in-command and the big sergeant-major the Gulag rats called 'Teeth' were already out there, waiting for him, staring at the flaming sky, ducking instinctively every time another shell crashed home, making the very earth beneath their feet tremble.

Katukov took in the myriad green and red signal flares hissing into the dark sky on the German side of the canal, always a sure sign that the Fritzes were launching an attack, and rapped out, 'Alert the battalion, Major!'

'Already done, Comrade Colonel,' the Marshal answered, his face tense and anxious in that eerie glowing light. 'I've alerted the reserve company, too.'

'*Horoscho!*' Katukov barked. In spite of being a traitor, Boldin was a very efficient soldier. 'But it looks as if we're not going to be hit this night. At least for the present.'

The Marshal did not argue with the NKVD colonel. Why should the Fritzes attack the Battalion's neighbours who occupied the same sort of defensive position they did, but were much further from their key objective, Moscow? No, there was more to the German plan that that. Instead he said urgently, 'With the Colonel's permission, I'd like to make a personal reconnaissance of the other side?'

Katukov looked at him hard.

The Marshal grinned. 'Don't worry, Comrade Colonel. It's hardly wise to attempt to desert in the middle of an attack, if that is what you are thinking. Your usual front swine is normally inclined to shoot first and ask questions later. I'd just like to know if the Fritzes are massing anything opposite us.'

'All right, I have other problems,' Katukov snapped, raising his voice as a battery of 155mms opened up to the south, their shells tearing the night sky apart with a great ripping sound. 'You have my permission. But I want you back at headquarters by dawn.'

'Thank you.' The Marshal wasted no more time. 'All right, Teeth, and you, too, Tinleg, let's make dust.'

'It's allus us poor cripples who land in the shit,' the little corporal protested, but unslinging his tommy gun, he followed willingly enough. A moment later the glowing gloom had swallowed them up.

The three Russians lay in the frozen bushes on the far bank of the canal, trying to ignore the racket on both flanks, eyes trying to penetrate the inky gloom to their immediate front. All seemed quiet, yet the Marshal had an uneasy feeling that they were not alone out there. It was almost as if he could smell the Fritzes. 'What do you think, Teeth?' he whispered.

He caught the dull gleam of the huge NCO's stainless-steel teeth reflected in the pink light from the south and then Teeth whispered, 'They're out there, Comrade. No mistaking that. Yer —' He broke off suddenly. 'There!' he hissed urgently. 'At two o'clock!'

The Marshal followed the direction of his outstretched hand, using the old campaigner's trick of bringing his gaze from the ground and focusing his eyes on the object at an angle. The Marshal caught his breath. The NCO was right. There was someone there!

'We go?' Teeth whispered.

He shook his head. 'No, we stay.'

'Shit!' Tinleg lying next to him on the snow cursed, but there was no fear in his voice, just anger.

Now they hardly dared breathe, as the thin line of dark shapes, boots obviously wrapped in rags so that they were almost noiseless, came closer and closer, bodies half crouched, as if they too were tense, frightened and apprehensive.

'Ten more metres,' the Marshal hissed. 'Then we open up… One burst and then run like hell.' Carefully he laid out their grenades in front of him in the snow.

The seconds ticked by in leaden, fearful apprehension. Now they could make out the Germans' strength. There were twenty of them. Too large for a normal patrol, the Marshal knew. What were the Fascists up to?

Abruptly they changed direction and started to slot towards the bushes where the Russians were hidden. The Marshal, his heart beating like a triphammer, his breath coming in short, sharp excited gasps, knew they'd be discovered in a moment. Raising himself on his knees, first grenade clasped in his right hand, he cried at the top of his voice, 'NOW!'

The grenade sailed through the air. It burst right at the head of the patrol. In the angry violet burst of flame, the Marshal caught a frightening glimpse of men flying through the air and the next instant Teeth gave a great bellow and pressed the trigger of his tommy gun. It burst into frenetic life. □

'*Ai-i-i!*' The scream of absolute agony seemed to go on for ever. The Germans were galvanized into frantic action, arms and legs twitching and writhing maniacally as that deadly burst of fire smacked into their defenceless bodies at such close range that they were thrown on to the snow like bloody, broken dolls.

Tinleg was not idle either. Doubling forward, as fast as he could with his artificial leg, he dropped on one knee to the right of the ambushed patrol and poured a burst into their rear.

The German attempting to set up a light machine-gun there went down choking in his own gushing blood, his face a red pulp. Tinleg fired again. His number two went down, almost sawn in half, his intestines pouring out obscenely on to the cold snow. Frantically his hands clutched at them, but they slid wetly through his fingers to hang there smoking horribly. Not for long. Tinleg's next burst whipped him right off his feet and flung him back against the nearest tree.

The Marshal raised himself and flung his last grenade, already aware of the shouts of rage and the shrill blasts on angry whistles further away. It was time to be off.

It burst in a blaze of scarlet flame just beyond the slaughtered patrol, missing the running survivors by metres, but illuminating the dark ugly shape concealed up to then by the grove of firs; and then they were running back to the frozen canal, angry white tracer zipping flatly through the glowing gloom and stitching a frightening pattern at their flying heels. But even as they ran for their lives, the Marshal's brain was occupied with what he had just seen. Why had the Fascists positioned a tank so close to the canal?

'Tanks, Boldin?' Katukov snapped, as the faint dirty white of the false dawn started to flush the sky to their rear. 'Quite impossible!'

The Marshal put down the glass of tea, laced with vodka that that big rogue Teeth had managed to "organize" somewhere or other, and said angrily, 'Comrade Colonel, I know a damned tank when I see one.'

Katukov took his eyes off the silent canal front, with beyond it the German positions still cloaked in thick darkness. 'All right, I'll accept your identification. Perhaps the Fascists have got one dug in there in a hull-down position as additional fire-power, just in case *we* attack across the canal?'

The Marshal laughed hollowly. 'I'm afraid with the state the Battalion is in that must remain a pious hope, Comrade Colonel. We are not going to attack, we are going *to be* attacked.'

'But how the devil are they going to get tanks across the Canal, Boldin?' Katukov demanded in irritation. 'Be reasonable, man. It's quite impossible.'

'Is it? That ice out there is pretty thick.'

'Thick enough to bear the weight of a Fascist tank, running to some thirty-odd tons?' Katukov sneered. 'Now surely, even you don't believe in such things, Boldin?'

'Always expect the unexpected, Comrade Colonel. It is one of the cardinal principles of warfare and has been ever since Hannibal crossed the Alps with his elephants in the depth of winter.'

'Elephants, that might be about the size of it. Now,' Katukov dismissed the matter of the tanks, 'I think we can safely stand down the first two companies till this evening. It looks as if our neighbours to north and south have got the situation well in hand.' He grinned unpleasantly at the angry Marshal. 'I don't think we can expect anything to happen at Krasnaya now except another long, cold, boring day. We can even rule out Hannibal's elephants, don't you feel?'

And with that he was gone, striding purposefully back to his *isba*, leaving the Marshal staring at his straight, broad back in impotent fury.

CHAPTER 4

'*Hals und Beinbruch!*' Manteuffel yelled above the ever-growing roar of the Stuka's motors, as the leading plane prepared to taxi across the snowbound field towards the tower.

Staffelkapitän Sturm's eyes lit up behind his thick goggles and then, pulling down his flying helmet, he prepared to take off, as the first green signal flare, fired from the tower, ascended into the dark dawn sky.

Manteuffel tugged his coat closer to his skinny undersized frame, as the prop wash caught it and tried to tear it from him. 'All right, Heinz,' he cried, 'I think we've done enough for the fly boys, don't you. Better be off!' Heinz took his eyes off the dive-bombers with the gull-like wings, as they started to bounce after Sturm towards the tower, and nodded his agreement. 'They look a good bunch of boys, General,' he commented as the two of them began to walk to the waiting staff car, 'that is, for the *Luftwaffe*, I mean.'

Manteuffel smiled. There was little love lost between the *Luftwaffe* and the Army. 'They're the finest pilots old Fat Hermann still possesses.'

'They'd better be, sir,' Heinz replied.

'What's that supposed to mean, Heinz?'

'Well, sir,' the aide-de-camp answered, his handsome young face suddenly worried, 'I was just thinking that if one of those flyboys missed the Popovs with his bombs, he might well just drop them on the canal and then that would be the end of the attack across the ice.'

'Nonsense, Heinz,' Manteuffel said easily, as they got into the car. 'They're the cream of the *Luftwaffe*. Sturm assured me that his boys could drop a bomb on a five-mark piece if called upon to do so. They won't miss.' Heinz said nothing.

Behind them the Stukas were gaining height rapidly, circling around the snowbound emergency field one by one until they reached Sturm who hovered above them like a black sinister hawk, seemingly almost stationary.

Manteuffel craned his neck to look at them, then he beamed. 'I rather pity the Popovs really,' he said. 'First the air attack and then the tanks. It's going to be one surprise after the other for them. Frankly, I don't think the poor bastards have got a chance, eh, Heinz?'

Still the young aide-de-camp said nothing.

General von Manteuffel shrugged imperceptibly: young men were a strange breed. Then he dismissed Heinz from his thoughts and concentrated on the great victory which would soon be his.

The blood-red ball of the sun hung on the horizon, bathing the steppe an eerie orange and throwing everything into harsh stark relief. Sturm in the lead noted it with approval. It was ideal bombing weather. Manteuffel had briefed him well enough of the danger to the whole operation that an accidental bomb dropped on the ice would cause. Now in that light they couldn't miss. They'd bomb the hell out of the Popov positions, but as soon as the target was obscured by smoke, he would call off his 'Black Hawks', as the dive-bomber veterans called themselves proudly. This day he would take no chances; the mission was too important.

Now he started to come down lower, the plane dragging a sinister black shadow behind it across the surface of the snow. His men followed suit.

Sturm grinned and began to hum that song he always unconsciously hummed when action was imminent: 'Do you see me, soldier, high in the sky... Do you ask me then whither I fly? I fly to far battle. I fly to death and blood's high shrieking. And, soldier, soldier, I will return, when death is dead...'

Ahead of him he saw the dull gleam of the Volga Canal with beyond it the brown patches in the snow which he knew indicated the foxholes and bunkers of the Russian line. He pressed his throat mike, ignoring the brown puffballs of the Soviet flak and white zipping tracer which now started to come his way. 'Sturm to Black Hawks,' he called, 'Sturm to Black Hawks ... going into the attack *now!*'

He pulled back the stick and pressed the throttle. The Stuka zoomed upwards, followed by the rest. At one thousand metres he levelled out and throttled back. For one long moment he seemed to hover there, a frightening metallic hawk, searching for its prey. He waggled his wings. The others knew the signal. He was going in for the attack. Sturm flicked on the wing sirens and then abruptly he dropped out of the sky, motors and sirens howling terrifyingly. Now he seemed to be heading straight for destruction, diving for the ground at five hundred kilometres an hour, gravity pressing his body hard back against the seat, his face behind the goggles and helmet flattened by the pressure, mouth wide open to prevent his eardrums from bursting. Down and down, the white earth leaping up to receive him, flak exploding all around him uselessly. Would he never level out?

At the very last moment when it seemed that a crash was inevitable, he jerked back the controls. The Stuka staggered visibly. The fabric screamed under that tremendous strain. And then from its ugly blue-painted belly, the myriad tiny but deadly black eggs started to tumble down towards the Soviet positions in crazy hectic confusion. The dive-bombing attack had commenced.

'*Hit the dirt!*' someone screamed frantically above the howl of the planes and the shrill whistle of the bombs. '*Hit th* —'

Thunder flowered all around the Punishment Battalion's positions, violet flame its stamen. Snow, frozen clods of earth, uprooted trees erupted, clawed agonizingly at the shocked, trembling air and collapsed, showering the terrified men huddled in their holes with dirt and steel shards.

A second stick hit the 333's line. The snow-covered earth quaked and trembled. Black earth spewed upwards. Everywhere men screamed out in terror and agony. A severed head, complete with helmet, rolled away like a football abandoned by a careless child.

Now another Stuka dived, engines roaring, sirens howling, falling out of the harsh blue winter sky as if to its own destruction. Red and white tracer zig-zagged purposelessly behind the stark black hurrying shape. It shuddered to a halt as if it had hit an invisible wall two hundred metres above the ground. The air was filled immediately with the whine of its bombs and the hoarse, chattering venom of the anti-aircraft machine-guns.

The Marshal ducked quickly. The bombs exploded with an ear-splitting crash. The big officer felt the ground rise and smash into his face. Something hot and salty streamed from his smashed nose. His own blood. He ignored it as the fist-sized, red-hot shards of steel hissed frighteningly through the trembling air. A shock wave of hot blast hit him in the face like a blow from a flabby fist. His lungs felt they must burst. He gasped frantically for air. All around him there were the curses and screams and cries for help of Gulag rats buried in the steaming earth. But at that moment no help was forthcoming. The survivors were too concerned with their own safety, feverishly burying themselves ever deeper into their pits before they became their graves.

And still the air attack went on. Time and time again they came hurtling down, sirens howling, bombs spilling from their evil bellies. One of the Black Hawks, carried away by the heady excitement of the kill, pulled out of his 500kmph dive too late. He smacked the ground at a tremendous speed. The Stuka shattered into a myriad pieces, snuffed out like some gigantic candle. Bombs swamped the line and the world rocked crazily, the whirling gale of metallic death and destruction sweeping the ashen-faced, terrified men so that they screamed silently, sickened by that hellish sound.

By sheer effort of naked willpower, the Marshal forced himself to raise his head above the level of his foxhole, alerted by another sound that somehow or other stood out apart from the snarl and howl of the diving planes. He stared across the jumbled mess of twisted equipment and severed limbs steaming with the heat of the explosions and settling into pools of congealed blood, ignoring the screams of men trapped in their holes, over the canal at the woods beyond. Was it coming from there? And what was it? Could it be —

His heart missed a beat.

The first ugly squat shape of a tank had begun to emerge from the firs. Bending them back to both sides, so that its deck was showered with falling snow, its long overhanging 75mm cannon swinging slowly from right to left, it looked like some metallic primeval monster seeking out its reluctant prey. Behind it, another Mark III started to crash its way out of the cover and with tracks churning up a wake of whirling snow commenced its way down to the canal below. Instinctively the Marshal knew he had been right and Katukov wrong. The Fritzes *were* going to attempt to cross the frozen ice! That was what the air-raid was being used for. To drown the noise of their motors and to make the defenders keep their heads down until it was too late.

'*Too late!*' The words flashed through the Marshal's brain with alarming electric suddenness. He had to do something. He did not hesitate. Ignoring the steel whizzing through the crazy air on all sides, he pulled himself out of his hole and pelted across the steppe, springing over dead bodies, wading through great smoking craters, clawing his way through the debris and the mangled equipment, and dropped into the log-covered command bunker. Katukov swung round startled, while the terrified young radio operator slumped over his set, head cradled in his arms like a frightened child trying to shut out some noise which scared him, sobbing heartbrokenly. 'You... What is it?'

The Marshal wiped the dirt from his face and gasped, 'The Fritzes, they're advancing with tanks.'

'Impossible!'

'Go and look for yourself, if you don't believe me. There were three of the Fascist bastards out there just now.'

'But the ice. It won't hold them, Boldin. I've already told —'

'Listen,' the Marshal yelled, cutting him short brutally, 'for better or worse, whether the damned ice holds them or not, the Fritzes are coming with tanks! That's the reason for this aerial bombardment. And we've got nothing to stop them!'

'The anti-tank rifles?' Katukov said, convinced by the other man's absolute certainty at last.

'Those pea-shooters! They'd bounce off the Fritzes' hide like ping-pong balls.'

'*Boshe moi*,' Katukov cursed, that hard, set face of his crumbling a little at the knowledge that if the Fascists broke through, Beria would not hesitate to carry out the final penalty. 'What are we going to do, Boldin?'

'There is only one way to stop them,' the other officer answered, as the bunker rocked under the impact of the bombs like a ship at sea, the daring plan beginning to form in his mind.

'How, man? Out with it, in God's name!' Katukov roared above the din.

Hastily Boldin explained, while the operator continued to sob, his shoulders heaving, the dirt and dust trickling down on his bare head unnoticed.

'But ... but...' Katukov gasped, 'that is impossible, absolutely impossible! You can't expect guns like that to be accurate. They haven't had a chance to range in. If they missed! God, it doesn't bear thinking about. Our whole line might be wiped out.'

'They'll be wiped out as it is, if we don't do something — *soon*! Listen.' The Marshal cocked his head to one side.

Katukov did the same.

For one long moment he heard nothing but the din made by the dive-bombers and then he heard it, the rusty rattle of many tracks.

'Tanks?'

Boldin nodded grimly.

'But the risk —'

Boldin waited no longer. Striding forward, he pushed the sobbing operator to one side and grabbed the earphones and mike himself. 'Here Sunray,' he rapped, 'here Sunray... Give me fire control...'

The die had been cast.

CHAPTER 5

The Mark IIIs waddled towards the canal like metal ducks moving towards a pond. Now the last of the Stukas was winging its way high into the hard blue sky in order to reach its fellows, leaving behind a scene of death and destruction in the loud echoing silence. Manteuffel, standing in the open turret of the lead tank, careless of his own safety, pumped his right hand up and down rapidly several times; the infantry signal for speed.

The great V of tanks moving down the snowy bank, throwing up a white wake behind them, increased their speed. Manteuffel narrowed his eyes against the sudden wind. So far there was no movement from the other side. Sturm's Stukas had done their work well. The Popovs were still lying bemused in the mess of great brown smoking craters which looked like the work of some gigantic mole. With a bit of luck, the tanks would be into their positions before they had recovered from that tremendous pounding. He flung a quick glance behind him. After each tank there came its "grape", a small cluster of crouched cautious infantrymen, each soldier with his rifle at the ready, face set in a grimace against the flying snow churned up by whirling tracks. Manteuffel nodded his head in satisfaction. The stubble-hoppers would take care of the Popovs once the tanks had carried their positions. Within the hour they would have overrun Krasnaya and be rolling through Tsaritsyn Res straight for Moscow itself. Instinctively he touched his collar at the thought and Heinz, crouched next to him in the turret, grinned amused. The Old Man was already imagining he had cured his throat-ache, a Knight's Cross of the Iron Cross worn around it.

'Anything funny, Captain?' Manteuffel asked icily, as the command tank lurched violently and then dropped on to the ice.

Heinz's grin vanished as quickly as it had come. 'Nothing, *Herr General.* Just thinking of something.'

'Don't think. It's not good for junior officers,' the little general snapped. 'Concentrate on the task —'

He broke off abruptly. A stab of scarlet had sprung up from the enemy line. A glowing white ball zipped across the ice, dragging a bright shadow after it, and it was heading straight for the command tank. 'Duck,' he yelled urgently.

The aide-de-camp ducked. In that same instant the miniature shell hit the side of the turret. There was the great hollow clang of steel striking steel. For a brief moment the inside of the turret glowed a dull red and then with a howl the shell, unable to penetrate the thick turret armour, howled away into the distance. Heinz grinned.

'Bounced off just like a table-tennis ball, sir.'

Manteuffel grunted, 'Let's hope that's all they've got in the way of A.P.' He seized the periscope and swinging it round hastily surveyed the Soviet positions. Nothing, save here and there the long-barrelled old-fashioned anti-tank rifles. He breathed an audible sigh of relief. Those particular can-openers were not going to be able to prise open his type of tin can. It looked as if he were going to pull it off after all.

Now twenty tanks were on the ice, spread out as Manteuffel had ordered so that their weight would be evenly distributed. The opposite bank was only thirty metres away and in spite of the ever-increasing volume of Soviet fire, nothing seemed to be able to stop them. Manteuffel took a last glance through his periscope and breathed out, satisfied. 'Give them another minute, Heinz,' he announced confidently, 'and the gentlemen from the Soviet paradise will be legging it for all they're worth.' Heinz grinned back at his chief. 'It certainly looks like it, sir. Moscow here we come!'

The Marshal bit his bottom lip with frustration as the white A.P. bullets howled off the advancing German tanks. Would the guns never open up? The Fascists were only a matter of metres away from their side of the canal now.

'If you want to know, brothers, whether you've got a cool head or not,' Teeth was saying to the rest of the men crouched in the front-line bunker, 'feel your salami. If it's hanging down, your nerves are all right. Go on — grab a handful of it.' He suited the action to his words and grabbed the front of his trousers crudely. 'See, I'm as cool as cream on a winter's day.'

'Mine's shrunk up, Comrade Sergeant,' someone said. 'Yes, that's because you're shit-scared,' Teeth commented, seemingly oblivious to the violent death which was almost upon them.

'I can't find mine at all!' Tinleg yelled above the rattle of the tanks. 'What's wrong with me?'

'Wrong with you? Hell, you didn't have a salami in the first place, Tinleg, you — little cripple!'

Tinleg and Teeth laughed at the joke, but the others remained unsmiling now. The tanks were almost upon them, the roar of their engines getting louder by the second. On the flanks the massed machine-guns opened up at Katukov's command, trying to dislodge the Fritzes sheltered behind the metal monsters. Here and there a German infantryman staggered or fanned the air wildly with his hands as he was hit, but the rest came on, obviously confident that victory was just within their grasp.

The Marshal flung a wild glance over his shoulder. The steppe behind him was empty of activity. The second-line troops had already fled, knowing that it was hopeless to attempt to fight tanks with infantry weapons. □

Was the Punishment Battalion going to be sacrificed in its first action, purposelessly, without even a chance of striking back? The Marshal slammed his clenched fist angrily against the sandbagged parapet of the trench. '*Damn, damn, damn!*' he cried with impotent fury.

The first tank started to approach the bank, its driver revving the engine violently as he prepared to climb. The Marshal could see the black and white cross on its turret quite clearly and the white blur of the driver's face through the open hatch. Would the guns never fire?

Suddenly the whole horizon to their rear quaked. Furious red lights blinked like enormous blast furnaces. With a hoarse exultant scream the first great 155mm howitzer shell ripped through the sky. Another followed and another so that the men below automatically clapped their hands over their ears to drown that terrible elemental roar. With a huge explosion the first shell smacked down. Right on target! A great hole appeared in the ice. For what seemed an eternity the Mark III, its driver petrified with fear, teetered on its edge, while the tank commander and gunner flung themselves out of the turret only to be mown down by Colonel Katukov's machine-gunners, then slowly and inevitably it started to slide into the water, its tracks whirling vainly.

A huge cheer rose from the Soviet line as yet another shell pounded down, taking a tank with it, plunging it down into the icy depths below. And then, terror-stricken and panicked, the Germans attempted to flee. Furiously the drivers whirled their vehicles round, sliding and slipping on the smooth surface, crashing into each other in their fearful haste, sparks flying high in the air, attempting to escape before it was too late.

But that wasn't to be. Great cracks ran in crazy spider-web across the ice, widening ever larger by the instant, turning into huge gaping holes. A tank disappeared into one. Another, trying to avoid the hole, reversed with a screech of tracks through the "grape" of following infantry, running a bloody track of screaming injured and dying men through them. □

Manteuffel's driver halted. Next to the little general, Heinz's face was ashen with fear. 'General —' he began.

Manteuffel ignored him. Pressing his mike-button, as yet another huge shell plunged down on the ice, shaking the command tank violently, he cried at his own artillery commander somewhere to the rear, 'Counter-battery fire, man... For God's sake, let me have counter-battery fire at once! We're being slaughtered out here... At —'

The words died on his lips. His tank had given a terrifying lurch. From below in his metal compartment, the driver screamed, 'We're going in, General... I can't hold her...'

Manteuffel flung a glance over the turret, which was already beginning to tilt at an alarming angle. The front bogies, churning uselessly, were hovering over a great hole. He realized immediately nothing could save them now; the ice was already disappearing beneath their tracks. 'Bale out!' he ordered, fighting desperately to keep the panic from his voice. 'BALE OUT!'

He ripped the earphones from his head and swung himself expertly over the side of the turret, dropping lightly on to the ice, cracking on all sides. Heinz was a little too slow. He freed himself one instant later and dropped right into the path of a fleeing Mark III. The glacis plate knocked him from his feet, his arms flailing wildly as he tried to save himself. To no avail, he was swept underneath the churning tracks. Manteuffel, crouched on the ice, gasped with horror as the Mark III rattled past him. Heinz had disappeared, save for one thing: the bloody head flopping back and forth between the links in the suddenly red tracks.

'They're hoofing it!' Teeth cried exuberantly as the last of the trapped tanks disappeared in a great spout of water through the shattered ice. '*The Fritzes are running!*' He pressed the trigger of his tommy gun. A wild burst of 9mm slugs stitched the ice at the heels of the fleeing survivors.

The Marshal touched his arm, as the thunder of their howitzers finally ceased, leaving behind a loud echoing silence, broken only by the screams of the fleeing Germans. 'Let them go, Teeth,' he said gently, almost sadly, 'they've suffered enough.'

'Ah, brother,' the one-eyed Captain Livny said, 'they're men like us... They've had enough.'

To their rear Vulf, surprised that his hand was not trembling after his first taste of combat and a little amazed by the apparent softness of these so-called hard-bitten professional soldiers, made a quick note in his little black book. Colonel Katukov would be interested in it, he was sure. Perhaps there'd be a bottle of pepper vodka in it for him; he'd see.

And then Katukov himself appeared on the scene, striding boldly through that lunar landscape, littered with dead and shattered equipment, while the boom of dead barrage echoed and re-echoed around the circle of hills to their rear. 'All right ... all right,' he barked, coming to a halt, hands on hips, booted legs well apart like the supercilious Guards officer he had once been, 'stop congratulating yourselves. There is work to be done. New bunkers to be dug, weapon-pits to be re-sandbagged, wire to be strung… Come on now, you Gulag rats. The war's not over by a long chalk yet!' He glared at the Marshal, who held his gaze with eyes that revealed no emotion, neither fear nor hatred, save boldness, as if he were challenging him to object.

The Marshal remained silent.

'All right then, come on, move yer lazy butts. They'll be back. Never fear!'

The action at Bloody Krasnaya was about to enter stage two…

BOOK THREE: *THE BRANDENBURGERS*

'I want you to become a robber-band, my own special secret troops, ready if need be to fetch the Devil from Hell!'
Admiral Canaris to the Brandenburgers, 1939.

CHAPTER 1

'It's Father Christmas himself,' one of the gigantic SS aides-de-camp muttered to his companion as the little Admiral's car came to a stop outside the main hut of the Rastenburg HQ. If the white-haired Admiral, who had gained his nickname from the SS because of his shock of prematurely whitened hair, heard the remark, he gave no sign of it. His deep-set enigmatic eyes revealed nothing. Instead he opened the door of the Mercedes and let his twin dachshunds drop to the ground.

The SS officer who had spoken shook his head in awed amazement, 'Do you see that? He comes to see the Führer and he brings his damned lapdogs with him. How does he get away with it?'

His companion grinned, as the sallow-faced admiral, who looked a good ten years older than he really was, seized his briefcase and entered the hut, forgetting to return the salute of the two black-uniformed SS giants. 'Because he's Canaris, that's why,' he whispered.

Adolf Hitler, surrounded by his generals, most of them with the purple stripe of the Greater General Staff running down the side of their immaculate grey breeches, eyed curiously the admiral advancing towards him in an un-pressed uniform devoid of decorations (it was one of the Secret Service Chief's quirks to dislike military decorations, forcing his staff to take them off before reporting to him), the dogs yapping about his feet.

He knew so much about his *Abwehr* Chief, and yet so little. He knew Canaris was a patriot, yet at the same time he had been in contact with the British ever since war had broken out.

He knew that the admiral had helped him actively to achieve tremendous victories in Poland, the West, and in Africa so that now the New Germany stretched from the Channel almost to the Urals; yet at the same time Canaris was equally actively opposed to National Socialism and the Third. Reich. And he knew, too, though he would never be able to prove it, that in 1939 Canaris had been one of the plotters who had planned to assassinate him.

Yet, Hitler mused, as Canaris halted and raised his arm in salute, he knew nothing about the mysterious little man. What motivated him? What was the reason for his long-time playing of both sides of the fence? He didn't know.

He flapped up his arm to return Canaris's salute and extending both hands took the admiral's cold hand in his own. 'Welcome to Rastenburg, my dear Admiral,' he said with more enthusiasm than he felt. Today he needed Canaris; he would have to make a play for his services.

Speedily the *Abwehr* chief was ushered to a corner of the room, where there were several plain pine benches and wooden chairs, while Colonel-General Jodl, Hitler's pale-faced and pale-eyed chief-of-staff, cleared his throat and prepared to brief him.

'*Herr Admiral*,' he began at a nod from the Führer, 'we have achieved tremendous victories in Russia and have suffered tremendous losses too. Indeed, our losses number some one million dead and wounded — at a cost to the enemy of some three million.'

'Two million would be closer to the mark,' Canaris said softly. 'If my sources of information are correct, of course,' he added with the quiet confident air of a man who knows his information is unimpeachable.

Jodl coloured slightly. 'You might be right there, Admiral. Well, losses we have suffered, but victory is within grasping distance, but everything depends on our capturing Moscow before the winter really sets in —'

'Not only will the capture of Moscow give our troops the winter accommodation they need,' Hitler broke in eagerly, as usual unable to contain himself for long, 'but it will undoubtedly bring about the downfall of Stalin and his Bolsheviks. They will flee and the whole rotten structure of communism will collapse about their ears like a house of cards. You see, communism…'

Canaris no longer listened. Verbal diarrhoea as usual, he told himself contemptuously, ignoring the broadfaced "Austrian Corporal", as he called Hitler behind his back, and concentrating on the problem in hand. Already he guessed why he had been called here. They wanted something from him and he had an inkling of what exactly that might be. Somehow or other they had learned about his own secret task force. They wanted the Brandenburgers…

The Brandenburgers, doomed men all of them, isolated fighters without the protection of international law, liable to be strung up from the nearest tree by the enemy if they were caught, had been raised in 1939, mainly from German-speaking Czechs, who had belonged to the illegal Storm Troop organization. It had been known as the German Company for Special Missions and had its depot at Brandenburg-on-the-Havel, which had given it its name.

By the end of the year the special formation, designed for clandestine operations behind enemy lines, had grown to battalion strength and Canaris addressing them that December had declared: 'I want you to become a robber-band, my own special secret troops, ready if need be to fetch the Devil from Hell!'

The secret unit, whose official existence was known only to the admiral himself, prepared for that mission in a manner completely new to the *Wehrmacht*. At "The Witches' Cauldron", as their secret training ground was nicknamed, they learned to speak foreign languages, to make parachute jumps, to make their own booby traps from fountain pens and matchboxes, and to survive behind enemy lines — for months, if necessary. Now the Brandenburgers were made up of a greater cross-section of German society than any other unit in the Army. Intellectuals with doctors' degrees rubbed shoulders with factory workers. German-American businessmen, who had slipped through the British blockade of the Atlantic, worked together with Germans who had spent most of their lives on South African farms or in the Australian outback and whose Afrikaans and English were better than their German. But whatever their background, the Brandenburgers were born adventurers and totally dedicated to "High C" as they called their chief.

In 1940 they had commenced their first missions. Disguised as Bedouins or British officers, Iraqi oil workers and Tibetan lamas, they had fought their war in the shadows over three continents, ranging from the icy wastes of the Finnish tundra and the trackless African desert to the glittering peaks of the remote Himalayas. And now, somehow or other, Hitler had got to know of their existence and the little Admiral, who would end his life hanging from a meat-hook, slowly choking to death as the SS guard pulled the chicken-wire ever tighter around his scrawny neck, could guess what the Führer wanted of him. His Brandenburgers were heading for Russia.

'…Therefore, as you can see, my dear Admiral,' Hitler was saying, 'everything depends upon our gaining a bridgehead over the Moscow-Volga Canal as soon as possible and then driving on towards the capital. As soon as the Reds commit themselves in the north, our panzers in the south will attack.' He brought his two hands together in one of those typically expansive gestures of his, raising and stamping down his right foot at the same time like a petulant child. 'Then we will crush them.' His flushed triumphant face darkened. 'But as yet we have not been able to force that damned canal. The Reds are stubborn swine, they are holding it with the greatest of determination. Forty-eight hours ago a mere battalion of them managed to throw back an attack by a whole German panzer division.'

'You mean General Manteuffel's, *mein Führer*?' Canaris said softly, knowing that it was always wise in Hitler's presence to appear to know more than one really did.

The Führer's dark eyes looked at him curiously. 'You are remarkably well informed, *Herr Admiral*.'

Canaris gave a stiff bow. 'It is the duty of the head of the Secret service to be well informed, *mein Führer*.'

'Of course. Now Canaris, the reason for my having summoned you here so hurriedly —'

'The front door cannot be forced and you expect me, sir, to steal in by the back one?' Canaris queried, noting out of the corner of his eye the shocked look on Jodl's and the other generals' faces. Very few officers succeeded in interrupting the Führer and getting away with it. Canaris did.

Hitler beamed. 'Exactly, *mein lieber Herr Admiral*. Exactly. I could not have put it better myself.'

Aware now definitely that Hitler knew of the existence of his Brandenburgers, Canaris wasted no time beating about the bush. 'You realize, *mein Führer*, that my — er — men are not the normal run of infantrymen, nor are they armed with any heavy weapons. Pistols, rifles and light machine-guns are the extent of their armament.'

'Of course, of course, Canaris. I understand that. But this would be a simple holding action until regular infantry came on the scene,' Hitler said hastily. 'The task of your men would be to surprise the enemy on the Volga Canal and allow General Manteuffel's people to cross undisturbed.'

'When?' Canaris rapped, his mind racing now.

Hitler looked at Jodl.

'Forty-eight hours at the most,' Jodl said after a moment's thought. 'Time is running out. The mercury is sinking rapidly. Soon it will be simply too cold for our soldiers to operate outside.'

'Forty-eight hours,' Canaris echoed. 'That gives me very little time to bring my people up from Brandenburg, brief them and get them into position for the kind of operation you envisage.'

'You can have any kind of transport you wish, Admiral,' Hitler said. 'The *Luftwaffe* is at your service. Junkers 52s are already waiting for you at Berlin-Tempelhof. You will have Priority Number One.'

'Army Group B has been alerted to render you every assistance,' Jodl added.

Canaris shook his wise old head, a plan already beginning to form in his brain. 'Thank you, *mein Führer*, and you, too, *Generaloberst*, but with your permission I like to do these things my way.'

'Then you are prepared to help Manteuffel in this matter?' Hitler exclaimed happily.

'Not just to help, *mein Führer*,' Canaris said confidently, picking up his briefcase, eager to be on his way to the airfield once more, 'but to succeed.' He stiffened to what he regarded as the position of attention, uniform crumpled and stained, shoulders hunched. '*Mein Führer, meine Herren*, I must be gone.'

And with that, not even waiting to receive the Führer's permission, he did just that, the dogs yapping happily at his feet, leaving the astonished officers and an equally astonished Hitler to stare at his vanishing back.

CHAPTER 2

'Have you ever thought,' Teeth said airily, 'that life's one big confidence trick, Tinleg?'

The corporal paused in the middle of picking his yellowing teeth free of the dried fish they had eaten at midday with his bayonet-point and asked: 'What do you mean, Teeth?'

Teeth took his time, his big brow furrowed, as if it were causing him some considerable effort to express his thoughts.

'Well, last month at this time, we were in the Gulag, working our nuts off for Uncle Joe and his crooks and hating every single breath he drew, the fat-arsed Georgian bastard.' He tugged the end of his nose routinely in case the freezing air might have some effect on it and spat drily on to the hard-packed snow outside the *isba*. 'Now we're saving the Motherland for him. Now who's the dummy there, I ask you?'

'Do yer want me to draw you a picture, Teeth?' Tinleg answered, staring at the empty horizon, bare of any kind of enemy activity for over twenty-four hours. '*You!*'

'Y're right there.' Teeth sighed and changed the subject. 'Wonder what the Fritzes are up to over there, eh, Tinleg?'

The little corporal followed the direction of his gaze. 'Who knows, Teeth, what the Fritzes are ever up to?' he said. 'Only thing I know is that they're up to no good, whatever it is.'

'Have you never thought of running across to them?' a new voice asked quietly. 'I mean those leaflets they keep firing across to us promise safe-conduct, good food — and women.'

The two NCOs turned to stare up at the newcomer, Vulf, the Battalion clerk. 'What did you say?' Teeth asked.

'I think you heard me correctly, Sergeant-major,' he said in that arrogant, drunken manner of his. 'What have Gulag rats like us got to lose?'

'We're Russian.'

Vulf laughed cynically. 'Do you really think, Sergeant-major, that that matters to those who command our destiny? Politicians are not Russian or German — or American for that matter. Politicians are politicians, a race apart, interested only in their precious little personal power. Patriotism means nothing to them.' He warmed to his subject, although he knew Katukov's order to him had been simply, 'Find out about the morale of those Gulag rats!'

'As you just said, Sergeant-major, last month we were criminals and traitors. This month we're heroes, patriots. Why?' He shrugged carelessly. 'Simply because they need us now.'

Teeth and Tinleg looked at him in surprised silence as he swayed there, bottle of pepper vodka raised to his frost-chapped lips.

'You talk a lot,' Tinleg said after a while.

'Yer, a lot of shit!' Teeth agreed. 'If our lot lie to us, do you think the Fascists are any better? Safe-conduct, good food and women — my hairy arse! What the Fascists have waiting for us is a slug at the back of the head, Vulf, that's what.'

Vulf grinned drunkenly. 'I 'spect you're right at that, Sergeant-major,' he said, slurring his words. 'Ours and theirs — they've both got us by the short hairs.' And with that he staggered off.

The problem of the right course of action also occupied the Marshal that long day of waiting. Sitting on a wooden ration box facing Livny, he poised, pistol in hand, ready for the rat which plagued the dug-out to reappear. He, too, wondered what should be done now that they had apparently defeated the Germans. 'It seems,' he said carefully, almost as if he were talking to himself, 'as if we've beaten them here, at least for the time being.'

Livny nodded his agreement, his one eye scouring the corners of the dug-out for the rat which plagued them so much at night, running over their faces, poking in their bread bags and, if they braved the cold enough to take off their boots, even nibbling tentatively at their toes.

'The question now is what they are going to do with the Battalion and how we officers are going to protect the men from being wasted as mere cannon-fodder? After all, we have managed to keep casualties fairly low up to now.'

'Ten per cent,' Livny said, as always right up to date with the latest information. 'We could go over to the enemy with the whole Battalion?'

The Marshal was silent for a moment, as if he might be seriously considering the idea. 'We'd be exchanging one camp for another.'

'But we'd be alive.'

'Agreed, but somehow, Livny it goes against the grain to go over to the Fritzes.'

Livny laughed easily and tugged at his eye-patch. 'Marshal, I do believe you're still a patriot.'

The tall, hard-faced officer, who had suffered so much under the Communists, joined in the laughter. 'I'm afraid I am — at least I'm a Russian, and — well, you know.'

'Yes, I know.' Livny pursed his lips. 'I've been thinking — if we could only educate Katukov!'

'What do you mean, educate him?'

'Well, he seems such a cold, unyielding swine, who hates our guts with a passion. Yet he is a good soldier and he appreciates us as good soldiers too, though his constant use of "Gulag rats" to us is not what I would call flattering.'

The Marshal smiled. 'I agree.'

'If we could only convince him that although we no longer share his political creed, we are patriots and Russians, ready to fight for our country to the last breath if necessary, then I think we could give him the necessary backbone to fight against those swine in Moscow the next time they want to send us off on a one-way mission.' The Marshal considered for a few moments, already aware of the faint sound of clawed feet. The rat was coming. 'I've seen such men before, Livny,' he said finally. 'They are loners, with no one to whom they can express their innermost thoughts, their fears, their hopes, their problems. They are men who hide their own uncertainty beneath an iron mask. In my experience they are unapproachable. How does one get through to a man like Katukov, I ask you that?'

But before Livny could answer that question, the rat appeared right at his feet. The Marshal didn't hesitate. He pulled the trigger. The dug-out rang with the sudden noise. Livny started. At his feet the rat, its head almost blasted away by the 9mm slug at such close range, lay still.

The sound of that single pistol shot at such close range startled Colonel Katukov. Suddenly flushed and guilty at what he had been about to do, he took the pistol from his mouth, wiped the moisture from its snub-nose carefully and slid it hastily back into the holster, looking around to check if anyone might have seen him.

'*Boshe moi*!' he cried to himself angrily, staring at his flushed features in the metal shaving mirror hanging on the wall of his dug-out. 'What kind of weak fool are you? Trying to do something like that — the coward's way out!'

He rose to his feet and started to pace up and down, shoulders and head bent in order not to bump into the low timber roof. □

He had never been a coward, neither to save himself from unpleasant consequences nor for political advantage. Of course, he had been scared often enough, but he had never been a coward. Wasn't it because of that virtue (or was it vice?) that his career had been ruined and he was here today, commanding a battalion of jailbirds, instead of an elite NKVD Division or one of the new "Stalin Scholars" formations as a full general?

Vera, his wife, had called him a fool when she had heard what he had done. Local Party secretary and senior doctor as she was, in the city where they had lived at that time, she had divorced him immediately. He had met her only once after that. She had been living with a cropped-haired, heavy-bosomed area Party secretary who affected male clothing and smoked cigars, and it was obvious what the two women's relationship was. Indeed, she had dismissed him contemptuously after five minutes with, 'Now I know what a fool I've been, living with you for five years.' Her eyes had blazed and the party secretary, a knowing smirk on her pudding face, had patted Vera's hand with her own tobacco-stained, bitten-nailed paw reassuringly. 'Now I know what *real* love is!'

Had he been a fool? Katukov paused in his pacing. Perhaps, but he had not been a coward. No, coward he had not been.

He recollected, with a sense of total recall, suddenly, that day in 1940 and the Poles…

The woods had been hot, terribly hot, so much so that he had been given permission by the senior commissar to allow his men to remove their jackets as they squatted there behind the line of machine-guns at the edge of the fir woods, waiting for they knew not what.

He had dabbed the sweat from his streaming brow and turned round to view the battlefield which was now Poland. Death and destruction stretched to the horizon. Shattered trucks, burnt and twisted tanks, blackened and torturedly tangled heaps of wreckage were scattered everywhere; and everywhere, too, rifles were thrust vertically, bayonet down, into the earth to indicate the dead who lay there.

He took his eyes off that great rubbish heap of metal and human flesh, the smashed skull, the ripped-apart belly with the viscera swelling out of it like some obscene sea plant, the already rusting piece of shrapnel protruding from an upturned throat, and gazed at the men emerging from the forest.

It had been a broad, dark-grey crocodile shuffling through the baking dust, giving off a subdued hum like that from a beehive, ten broad — the end of the column of Polish prisoners out of sight, there were so many of them.

All the misery of human existence had seemed to be concentrated at that moment in those staggering, lurching men, urged on by the whips and curses of the riders, their naked feet or battered boots throwing up a cloud of dust so that they had seemed to be legless, floating through the stifling air.

Someone had bellowed an order. Perhaps it had been the General. Now, he knew the guards on horseback had known what was to come. He hadn't. Then. They had urged their ponies into a gallop and had abandoned that pitiful column hurriedly, lashing the animals' steaming, sweat-glistening backs, leaving the prisoners to stand or slump there, dull-eyed and fatalistic, not even caring what might well happen to them.

Again someone cried an order. This time he had known it had to be the General. Who else would have dared to have given such a terrible order? Almost at once the machine-guns at the far end of the NKVD line had commenced chattering. He had stared incredulously as the Poles began to fall. There had seemed no urgency about it. The Poles had been too weary even to scream or fight to back away from that merciless fire. They had fallen where they had stood, no expression on their faces save perhaps one of resignation, even relief, that the misery was finally over.

The bodies had piled up and up like the heaps of logs he remembered in the great forests of his homeland as a child, stacked by the sweating loggers. Ever more and more: the powder-stained, panting gunners had clambered up the heaps of corpses and set up their machine-guns once more to commence firing at those huddled beyond and still alive. He had followed numbly, as if in a dream, not even nauseated by this terrible slaughter, which had happened so suddenly, watching it as if it might have been some newsreel dealing with events taking place at the other side of the world.

It had been then that the Polish general had stepped forward. He had been a slight man, dwarfed by one of those silly capes the Poles insisted on wearing, his face under the gold-braided, three-cornered hat pale, but set and determined. He had held up his hand, as if commanding the gunners to stop, ignoring the bullets cutting through the air all around him, and said something in Polish. Then in broken Russian he had added, 'Comrades, we are soldiers too, you know.'

Broken the Russian might have been, but those simple words had had such a noble majesty about them, that he, Katukov, had realized immediately that this massacre, for that was what it was, could not go on. Seized by a sudden impulse, he had rushed to the front of the line and screamed 'Stop … stop … for God's sake, *stop firing!*'

Of course it had been to no avail. They had stopped for a few moments until their own general had come running up, his fat belly wobbling, his moon-face crimson and running with sweat at the effort. 'Katukov, have you gone mad, man!' he had bellowed, spraying the colonel's impassive face with spittle in his rage. 'In God's name, don't you realize I could have you court-martialled for this? The order to deal with the Polack fascist imperialists comes from Comrade Beria personally.' Without waiting for Katukov's reaction, he had swung round and screamed: 'Commence firing… Damn your eyes, you gunners, commence *firing at once!*'

With a fat hand that trembled violently he had aimed at the lone Polish general and fired. His aim had been inaccurate and the Pole went down on one knee, bleeding from a bullet in the lower leg. The NKVD general had fired again. This time he hit the Pole in the gut. Katukov had heard his grunt of pain quite clearly. Still he hadn't gone down altogether until the nearest machine-gun had begun to fire once more, slicing off the top of the man's head. Then he had gone down for good.

The place had been Katyn and that hot day nearly ten thousand Poles had been massacred in cold blood and buried secretly in the woods. It was a name that he would bear with him to his grave, for the events at Katyn had ruined his career, his life and his future. Then, as now, he had known with the clarity of a sudden vision that it had marked him indelibly as a man branded by fate. Wasn't it, therefore, better to put an end to it now, end this miserable existence, while he still had some honour left?

Again, almost of its own volition, his right hand slid down to his pistol holster and felt the cool reassuring comfort of that butt which could solve all problems once and for all. Should he?

But that solution was not to be realized this day. Like a sudden gale of wind, the storm of shells broke over the Punishment Battalion's positions and the dug-out was groaning under the impact as the first salvo thudded into the frozen ground above. '*Alarm … alarm*,' the frightened voices outside bellowed. 'Alarm'.

Abruptly the alarm bells were ringing everywhere and the field phones jingling, as racing feet pelted for the foxholes and dug-outs. The battle for Krasnaya had commenced once more.

CHAPTER 3

The whole of the circle of hills around the canal seemed to be on fire. It was as if some immense giant was shaking the whole world. *Crash … howl … plump.* The 155mm shells exploded in a terrifying howl, sending up huge mushrooms of flying earth. The mortar shells detonated with a ringing crack, spewing red-hot flying steel on all sides. And the rockets, nerve-racking, stupefying, flaming killers, showers of fiery sparks trailing behind them, crashed to the ground in spurts of fire like miniature volcanoes, engulfing everything in their life-destroying, searing heat. The very earth, as if mortally wounded itself, seemed to rear up in agony.

The defenders of the Volga Canal bank, caught in the heart of that seething hellish cauldron of shattering steel, huddled into small bundles, bodies trembling violently, fists pressed into their mouths in fear or clasped over their ears like children trying to keep out some terrifying sound, steel and pebbles clattering off their bent helmets.

On and on that terrible bombardment went. A great booming sledge-hammer of noise which slammed down time and time again. Without respite. The pits filled with dead, dying, and wounded drowning in their own gurgling warm blood. The living huddled together in fear, not realizing that they were shrieking with terror, their eyes coated with hot sheen, as if tears were near, their pinched, white-nosed faces ashen and drained of blood.

Men who had not prayed in a lifetime begged God to make the sun go down and give them respite from that awful pounding. Men became whimpering animals, not knowing how badly they had soiled themselves. Men went crazy, howling like wolves, teeth bared like fangs, held down only by the combined efforts of their comrades. Men took the only way out and with their naked toe crooked around the trigger of the rifle pressed up underneath their chins, blew their heads off.

And still that bombardment continued. Hour after terrible hour. The Punishment Battalion's positions were reduced to rubble. Their dead lay everywhere, with the living burrowing their way out of the shattered holes furiously to lie on the surface, spent and exhausted, chests heaving frantically like those of ancient asthmatics. Would it never stop?

The murderous inferno ceased as abruptly as it had begun. At first the dazed survivors would not believe that it had ended. They could scarcely conceive of such a blessed silence. Here and there the first hesitant survivor raised his head above the rim of his trench. Their eardrums thundered on of their own accord. Their hearts beat hectically, as if they had just run a race. Before them, marred by a mist of acrid powder and drifting smoke, there was a completely transformed landscape. Awed and wide-eyed they stared at it and then at each other, as if they were telling themselves 'we are the last creatures to inhabit the world' for that smoking scene was bare of human life, inhabited now solely by the dead, sprawled everywhere in the careless, abandoned positions of those who have been violently done to death.

Katukov wiped the dirt from his scummed, cracked lips and looked at Boldin. The Marshal returned his look, awed too by the great bombardment into momentary silence, as if the two of them had witnessed some tremendous act of the Deity himself.

Finally the colonel found his voice. 'What ... what do you make of it, Boldin?' he croaked.

The Marshal searched the other side of the canal and then the horizon before replying. 'I … I don't know, Colonel,' he answered, his voice seeming to come from a long way away, as if it didn't quite belong to him. 'I see nothing…'

'Neither do I.' Colonel Katukov bit his bottom lip with worry. 'But they don't fling a hate like that at us, Boldin, for nothing, do they?'

'No, no commander in his right mind, and that includes the Fritzes, would waste that amount of ammunition just to frighten his opponent, Colonel.'

'Agreed.' Colonel Katukov frowned at the horizon, as if challenging the enemy hidden somewhere or other there to cause trouble. 'But what's their ga —' He broke off suddenly, his normal self once more. 'Major, get every man of those Gulag rats of yours on the job. Evacuate the wounded. Build up the defences as best you can. No one to stand down… Get on with it now!' He flashed a glance at the sky. The winter gloom was already beginning to creep in from the east. In an hour it would be dark and when darkness came, he knew instinctively, the trouble, whatever it might be, would commence. 'Move it, Boldin, at the double now… There is no time to be wasted.'

The Marshal sprang out of the bunker. He knew Katukov was right. He could almost smell the tension in the air.

Boldin fired his fourth flare of the last hour. It sailed into the night sky, bathing the immediate area to their front in an icy white-glowing light.

Standing crouched next to the parapet together with Teeth and Tinleg, he peered across the gleaming silver line of the canal. But the enemy-held side of the waterway was still. There was absolutely no sign of movement in their positions. For all he knew the whole of the Fritz Army might well be fast asleep.

Boldin cursed softly to himself as the flare dropped slowly to the ground, cloaking everything in a thick darkness once more.

'Son-of-a-whore,' Tinleg grunted. 'Why can't the Fascists fight a proper war and let poor honest soldiers get a bit of shut-eye?'

'Poor you may be,' Teeth sneered, 'but honest you've never been.' His voice grew more serious. 'What do you make of it, Comrade Major?'

Boldin tugged his collar closer to his ears and shrugged. 'God knows. All I know, it's cold enough to freeze the eggs off you and the Fritzes are up to something. What, is beyond me. All right, I'm off to inspect the line again.' He handed Teeth the signal pistol. 'Fire one in a quarter of an hour's time and keep yer orbits peeled. They're up to something. I feel it in my bones.' The Marshal pulled himself out of the hole with a grunt and stamped off into the darkness, leaving the other two to continue their freezing watch, sunk in gloomy, frigid silence.

One kilometre to their rear, *Leutnant* Karst watched as that last flare fell to the ground to die in a final splutter of white flame and then turned to his Ukrainers, who were peeling off the last of their German uniforms to reveal the earth-brown Red Army smocks below. '*Davoi, tavorschi,*' he urged in his fluent Russian, which he spoke as well as his men's native Ukrainian, 'our

Popov friends are getting nervous down there. It's damn cold, too.'

Feldwebel Bogodan, his Ukrainian second-in-command and the Brandenburgers' most notorious skirt-chaser, grinned back at him in the darkness. 'Lieutenant,' he said, taking a final swig from the rum and tea mixture his canteen contained, 'there's only one place a sensible man should be on a night like this.'

'I know.' Karst beat him to it. 'In the hay cuddled to a big-titted wench.'

'Correct, Lieutenant.'

'When we finish this mission,' Karst said, rising to his feet, 'I'll see you get a whole whorehouse in Berlin full of them to satisfy your nasty lecherous tastes. I don't doubt old High C would be only too willing to pay for them.'

'He should,' Bogodan replied. 'After what we've been through tonight to get here, rowing across that shitting canal in a full-scale artillery bombardment and now risking being strung up on the nearest tree if the Red swine catch us in this uniform.'

'My heart bleeds for you,' Karst said in that careless, good-humoured, absolutely fearless manner of his, which had made him one of Canaris's most able young commanders. 'Now come on. Let's get out of here. It'll be dawn in another two hours. *Davoi!*'

In the next hour the Brandenburgers set about the destruction of the Russians' second line, burning, looting and destroying with impunity, catching the surprised troops unawares, slitting the throats of gun-crews, cutting down communication wires, mining the supply roads, booby-trapping parked trucks.

Karst was in his element, whispering exuberantly to Bogodan time and time again, 'We've got them with their knickers down, *Feldwebel,* and their legs apart!'

As dawn began to approach they had completed the task that Admiral Canaris personally had assigned them in Berlin. They had cut a great swath of destruction a kilometre broad and two deep to the rear of the Russians holding the canal. Now when the trouble started, the defenders of the canal could expect no immediate support from the rear, and by the time the Russian commanders further back became aware of the enemy in their midst it would be too late: the canal would be in German hands.

Karst was satisfied. As somewhere the first frozen rook began to caw hoarsely, indicating that first light was imminent, he gave his final orders to Bogodan. 'Half the men to set up the landing lights. The rest take up defensive positions.'

Bogodan hesitated only a fraction of a second. 'It'll be the give-away, *Leutnant,*' he said thoughtfully, tugging at his straggle of black beard. □

'Got to be, Bogodan,' Karst said as bold as ever. 'Anyway, they're going to know we're here pretty soon now. *Was soll's?*' he asked in his native German and shrugged. 'If things go wrong, we'll all be making pretty corpses, won't we?'

Bogodan sniffed and then, turning, rapped out his orders.

Hastily those with the lanterns separated into two files and running down the length of snow-covered steppe to their front, began under Bogodan's orders to place them at regular intervals. Intently Karst watched their dark shapes running through the pale gloom, praying that the snow concealed no rocks or boulders, then when the last lantern was in position, he took a deep breath before crying out at the top of his voice, for now there was no more need for concealment, '*Light 'em up!*'

Matches scratched against boxes. Everywhere along the two lines there were spurts of blue flame. One by one the petroleum lamps started to hiss furiously, bright red flames illuminating the darkness until all at once there was a great red arrow pointing, so it seemed, directly at the positions of the Punishment Battalion.

The Brandenburgers were ready for action.

CHAPTER 4

'In three devils' name — what's that?' the Marshal cried in alarm, as the red shaft of light stabbed the gloom a kilometre or so to the rear of their line.

For one moment, he thought it might have been some accidental blaze, some fool of a hash-slinger who had set his goulash-cannon on fire, or perhaps a flash-fire at an artillery ammunition dump; then he realized that that could not be. The flame was too regular, too perfect, too man-made. Hardly aware that he was doing so, he had his officer's whistle out in a flash and was blowing three shrill blasts on it.

'*Stand to ... stand to...*' the excited calls flew from dug-out to dug-out as the alarm bells rang and NCOs bellowed orders. Already tracer was beginning to hiss back and forth like a swarm of angry red hornets and there was that well-remembered, high hysterical buzz which the Marshal knew was the sound of a Fritz Spandau machine-gun firing 800 rounds per minute. With it, there came the knowledge that the Germans were now behind them. Somehow they had managed to cross the canal unseen. That fact seemed to numb him momentarily, as excited soldiers rushed to their posts, struggling into their equipment and helmets, clicking off the safety on their weapons as they ran.

'Boldin, don't just stand there, man!' Katukov's angry bellow woke him to reality once more.

He spun round. Katukov was standing at the entrance to his dug-out, careless of his own safety, body fully outlined by the yellow light streaming from within, pistol in his hand. 'Your orders, Comrade Colonel?' he cried.

'We can expect another crossing of the canal, Boldin. I'll take charge here. Take the reserve company and counter-attack. Clear the Fritzes —' He ducked hastily as a burst of machine-gun fire narrowly missed his head, stitching a pattern of sudden death in the sandbags above him. Ignoring the sand trickling from them and falling on to his broad shoulder, he continued with '— from that position. At once. Clear?'

'Clear, Comrade Colonel!'

As Katukov disappeared into the gloom to take charge of the line, Boldin cried at the waiting Teeth and Tinleg, 'After me, you two — at the double! Come on now!'

The three of them ran clumsily over the uneven surface of the snow to the *isbas* occupied by the reserve company. Already they were alerted, some of them crouching behind the poor protection offered by the ramshackle wood and stone structures, firing back at the defenders of that strange glowing arrow.

Boldin skidded to a halt. The officer who had complained about the loss of his middle finger was in charge of the company, ready and eager to go. Boldin gasped, 'Well, now you can get your own back, brother.'

The other man grinned nastily. 'Show me the way, comrade, just show me the way.' Then his grin vanished. 'What the hell do you think it's for?' He pointed at the arrow of light. 'God knows. All I kn —' The rest of the Marshal's words were drowned by the obscene belch of the enemy mortar. 'Hit the dirt!' he screamed frantically, as the dawn sky was torn apart by the howl of the descending bomb.

They flung themselves down. Steel cut through the air. Someone howled with pain. Boldin rubbed the snow from his face. 'Flank attack!' he commanded hastily, instinct telling him that the defenders of that strange light would have to be taken out soon before they could realize whatever mischief they were undoubtedly planning. 'You take half the company. I'll take the other half. Off you go!'☐

'Prepare to attack ... fix bayonets!' the Marshal yelled, feeling the old heady excitement of impending battle overcome him and the adrenalin pumping energy into his body frenetically.

There was the hush of steel being hurriedly withdrawn from metal scabbards.

The Marshal did not wait for them to report their readiness. Instead he unslung his round-magazined tommy gun and cried above the snap-and-crackle of the fire fight, *'Follow me!'* The ragged line of soldiers started to run from the *isbas* towards the lights, their greatcoats flapping around their flying ankles. *'Urrah!'* they cried, carried away by the excitement of the attack. *'Urrah!'*

The red-gleaming lights loomed up larger. The Marshal could see them quite clearly now. His finger curled around the trigger of his submachine-gun. Surprisingly enough the volume of fire directed against the running men had begun to slacken. Why? Suddenly a dark figure loomed up only ten metres away. He caught himself from pressing the trigger of his weapon just in time. The man was wearing Russian uniform. 'Hold your fire!' he sobbed. 'Hold your fire everywhere!'

'Comrade!' the stranger said, holding up his hands to show that he was unarmed.

The whole running line of men came to a halt. They stared at the man in the dirty smock of the Red Army. But not for long. Suddenly the man flung himself to the ground and yelled something in Ukrainian. A German stick grenade came hurtling from a ditch to their right.

'D —' The marshal's warning came a fraction of a second too late. The front rank of his gawping soldiers flew to all sides, torn apart by that terrible explosion at such close range.

'*Traitors!*' some screamed as they fell. 'Kill them!' others yelled. 'KILL!' Now the Marshal could not restrain his men. They streamed forward, their rifles tossed to one side, their hands clasping axes, knives, sharpened spades. Like a pack of wild animals, ignoring their own losses as the Ukrainian fire ripped their ranks apart, they fell upon them, slicing, hacking, slashing.

They had no mercy. Stumbling over their own dead and writhing wounded, they rained blow after blow on the Ukrainians' raised faces, the foam at their lips, muttering obscene curses, their eyes wild and glaring. Caught up in an elemental animal blood rage, they continued with their gory butchery till at last their crazed brains finally became aware of the strange hissing noise above their heads.

'Gliders!' the Marshal screamed fervently. 'For God's sake, stop that!'

'GLIDERS!' —

And then the first of the great silent planes came winging out of the grey dawn sky, sailing effortlessly over the heads of the men slaughtering each other on that blood-stained snowfield. Admiral Canaris had achieved his first surprise!

CHAPTER 5

'GLIDER!' the Marshal yelled fervently once again. Above him at no more than twenty metres' distance, the gigantic Dornier 230 seemed to fill the whole sky for a moment. And then it was past, the pilot tugging the blunt nose upwards to act as a brake, the wind howling through the slats of the wing-brakes, before he could loose off a burst at its tremendous, blue-painted wooden belly. It hit the snowfield and slewed to the right in a flurry of flying white. Just in time the pilot caught it. It straightened up and bounced ten metres back into the air. A second later it hit the ground again. One thousand kilos of men and material slithered forward at eighty kilometres an hour, the plane almost disappearing in the blinding-white wake of snow. One after another with cracks like pistol-shots, the barbed wire strands wrapped around its skids as extra brakes snapped. The fir forest loomed up in front of it. The Marshal caught his breath. Would the pilot be able to make it? Then, swaying and shuddering, one wing splintering like matchwood as it hit a boulder hidden by the snow, the plane came to a stop.

Almost immediately the men inside started to hack at the canvas walls with their knives and bayonets, while the Gulag men, prostrate in the snow, watched their efforts to escape as if mesmerized. The door flew outwards and a German stood there, his head adorned by the rimless helmet of their paratroopers. It was only then that the watchers came out of their trance.

The first burst ripped along the canvas side, stitching bloodstained holes its whole length. The German in rimless helmet pitched forward into the snow. Behind him other men appeared. The Gulag men concentrated their fire upon them. Stunned and confused by that tremendous volley of lead they spun and collapsed, tumbling out on to the snow like marionettes in the hands of a suddenly crazy puppet-master.

But now their fellows were cutting their way out of the fuselage, firing as they burst out of the material like murderous chicks emerging from their shells.

The Marshal flung his last grenade. It exploded with a sear of white phosphorus at the side of the glider. It went up in flame at once. Screams rose up from within as the survivors realized they were trapped by the flames.

'Don't let them escape,' the Marshal began, but his words were drowned by the screech of the next glider's skids as they struck the frozen surface of the snow.

The Marshal swung round to face the new enemy. He fired a burst from the hip automatically. The pilot's face disappeared behind a gleaming spider's web of shattered glass. He lost control. The great plane swerved to the right. It somersaulted to a stop, both wings broken off by the impact, its tail high in the air. But in spite of the terrible damage, men started to pour from the ripped fuselage, firing as they came, racing for the cover of the pits prepared for them by their Ukrainian comrades.

Another hit the ground, effectively covered by the thick black smoke and flame now surging ever higher from the burning first glider. A fourth followed it and a fifth.

With a sinking feeling, the Marshal raised himself from his own cover and cried, 'Move back, men ... move back ... fifty metres!' And even as he gave the order, he knew that Punishment Battalion 333 was in trouble now, serious trouble.

It was exactly ten minutes after the Brandenburgers' glider attack that all the infantry General von Manteuffel could muster from the 7th Panzer Division started to cross the canal, some dropping into the freezing water and, unburdened by anything but their weapons, striking out for the far bank, while others in groups pushed out the flat-bottomed, canvas-clad wooden assault boats.

Almost immediately Katukov's three companies reacted. His mortars ranged in at once, throwing up great spouts of water and whirling bodies as their shells struck home, as the bullets from the infantry smacked into the furiously paddling Germans in the little boats. But von Manteuffel, hating the way he would have to sacrifice his infantry in a frontal assault of this kind, had a few surprises to spring on the defenders all the same. In the lead-boats the combat engineers, crouching awkwardly on the blunt prows, knowing that if they were hit they would not stand a chance burdened as they were with the heavy fuel packs, pressed the triggers of their terrible weapons. Long tongues of angry red flame reached out for the opposite bank, igniting everything in their path, making the water boil abruptly, melting the snow to leave behind a smoking, charred surface to mark their passing. An instant later his tanks, dug in in a hull-down position beyond the crest of the hill, commenced lobbing their great 75mm shells into the Russian positions.

Now both sides began to take casualties. German after German screamed as he was hit and disappeared into the suddenly blood-red water, whipped up to a fury by the bullets striking the canal on all sides. Here and there a Russian defender, caught by that terrible, all-consuming flame and turned instantly into a human torch, broke from his position and ran screaming to the rear to throw himself into the snow.

Writhing back and forth in a vain attempt to put out that agonizing fire.

Now the canal was full of dead men floating face-downwards in the violent water and dying men fighting frantically to free themselves from their equipment before it dragged them under for good. But still the Germans kept on coming.

Now the first of their little boats, some of them laden with corpses lying in their own gore, nosed the opposite bank. The attackers clambered out of them and started to clamber up the steep slope, crawling over a carpet of their ever-new dead, screaming hysterically as they clawed their way through the frozen mud ever closer to the Russian positions.

Katukov, careless of his own safety, stood on the parapet of a bunker firing his submachine-gun and urging his men to ever greater efforts, the bullets tugging at his uniform. The defenders poured a hail of slugs into the first wave as it broke over the top to their front. Here and there the Germans threw their weapons away and raising their hands in surrender, croaked '*Kamerad ... nicht schiessen ... Kamerad!*' But death was greedy. It harvested them all with that steel scythe, cutting down those who fought and those who surrendered.

Katukov, old soldier that he was, knew now was the time to break them or lose his position. 'At them!' he called above the din of battle, 'At them, soldiers!'

'Forward brothers!' Livny cried. 'Forward!'

Still the men hesitated.

Katukov stared down at them in their pits contemptuously. 'Do you want to live for ever, you Gulag rats?' he screamed. 'You bunch of pimps and whoresons!'

The words had their effect. They broke from their holes. Now, glad to be relieved of that almost unbearable tension, hating the man who ran at their head with a burning passion, they streamed forward, screaming terrible obscenities.

The two bands of men smashed into each other with an audible crash. They fought where they stood in the frozen mud and rusting barbed wire, gouging out each other's eyes, stabbing and kicking, heavy, steel-shod boots smashing down on the opponent when he fell, turning his upturned face into a bloody featureless pulp, throttling one another with bare hands, and killing, killing, killing until in the end the attackers broke. Staggering back the way they had come, slipping and stumbling down the bank, they retreated to the boats, leaving the Russians too weak to follow them. Instead they tottered back to the safety of their own holes, chests heaving, faces ashen and sickened at that great slaughter, all energy drained from their skinny bodies, already aware from the ever-increasing and louder volume of fire to their rear that Major Boldin had been unable to deal with the glider-borne troops and that they were now trapped between two lines of the Germans.

CHAPTER 6

The Marshal wiped the trickle of dark-red blood from the bayonet slash across his right temple and took a grateful drink from the canteen of vodka that Katukov had handed him silently.

Outside there was quiet again, even the birds were singing joyfully as the pale yellow luminous ball of the December sun started to ascend higher into the light blue sky. Only the groans and moans of the wounded in the next bunker recalled the tremendous battle Punishment Battalion 333 had just fought.

Katukov took his gaze off the frozen churned mud, littered with bloody mutilated corpses of both armies, some with great holes ripped in their contorted bodies, as if some crazy surgeon had gone to work with explosives instead of a scalpel. 'Well?' he demanded.

The Marshal hesitated only momentarily. Boldly he replied, 'We haven't a chance of holding this position for longer than twenty-four hours.'

'You can't mean that, Boldin?'

The Marshal looked at Livny leaning against one of the charred timbers of the now roofless command bunker. 'Tell the Colonel,' he commanded.

Livny straightened up easily, like a man who had an untroubled conscience. 'Comrade Colonel, the Fascists have managed to hold a stretch of our side of the canal of about five hundred metres in length. As soon as night falls they will undoubtedly start building a pontoon bridge to bring across their armour. If they knew that we were without artillery and radio links to the rear, they would start building it now in daylight. Fortunately they don't know that.'

Katukov frowned, but said nothing.

'Behind us, I estimate from the size of those gliders that the Fritzes have landed some two hundred to two hundred and fifty men.' He looked at the Marshal.

Boldin forced a weary smile. 'Put it at two hundred, Livny. You know we were not just twiddling our thumbs out there. I think we accounted for a couple of the Fritzes before they chased off!'

'Two hundred, then. So, Comrade Colonel, it is not unlikely that we'll see the Fritzes behind us reinforced during the day, perhaps towards evening, by further airborne troops, while at the same time his armour will begin crossing the canal. Then —' Livny left the rest of his sentence unsaid, simply closing his two extended hands together to illustrate what he felt their fate might be.

'But the *Stavka* won't leave us to our fate,' Katukov protested. 'Even if we do not have radio communication, they'll realize what's going on up here.'

The Marshal indicated with a tilt of his head the direction from which the faint rumble of heavy gunfire was now coming. 'A feint is going on further north, obviously to keep High Command guessing. Besides,' he grinned maliciously at a worried Katukov, 'where are the reserves to come from? After all, isn't that the reason why Krasnaya is being defended at this very moment by Gulag rats like ourselves? There are simply no more bodies.'

Katukov bit his bottom lip, ignoring the jibe. 'What do you suggest, Boldin?'

'There is only one suggestion that any sane commander can make, Comrade Colonel.' And now there was sudden iron in the Marshal's voice.

'What is that?'

'Withdrawal while there still is time.'

Katukov looked at the other man with shocked eyes. 'You ... you can't mean that, Boldin?'

'I certainly can. We've lost a hundred men and have another hundred more or less seriously wounded. We have no artillery and no anti-tank weapons save those damned antiquated peashooters. We can't expect to hold off a fair portion of a German armoured division, especially with the enemy building up to our rear.'

'But the position, man, it's vital!'

'Colonel, generals have been saying that right throughout history.'

Boldin forced a laugh. 'Undoubtedly I've probably said it myself in the old days. But I have learned since then. It is not terrain that is important, Katukov, *it is men*! Terrain can always be recaptured, but men, once dead, can never return.' He stared hard at Katukov, while the guns to the north rumbled on. 'Retreat and live to fight another. Stay and fight — and we'll lose both the Battalion and Krasnaya.'

Colonel Katukov thought of that blazing hot summer's day in Poland and that look in the fat general's eyes when he had ordered the machine-guns to stop firing. Could he risk that kind of disgrace once more? It wasn't just Beria's threat; it was the thought that he had failed to carry out orders once again. Drawing in a deep breath, he made his decision. 'Major, Captain,' he glanced with his hard face set from Boldin to Livny, 'we will not withdraw. Krasnaya will be held to the last bullet and the last man...' Without giving them a chance to object, he rapped, 'Now dismiss!'

As if in a daze the two Gulag rats staggered outside, their eyes eloquent with defeat.

Morosely Teeth picked at the *Kavka*, nose wrinkled up in disgust at the taste of the cold porridge, filled with green insects that had come to the surface when it had been cooked and now lay there stranded and dead in the glutinous mess. 'What shit,' he commented.

Tinleg looked enviously across at the cold food; he had long finished his. 'Shit for shits, I say. But if you don't want it, Teeth, just shoot it over here. I'm not particular.'

Teeth spooned up a half-dozen green insects, closed his eyes momentarily and swallowed them hastily. 'It's food, I suppose,' he said thickly and then handed the canteen over to an eager Tinleg. 'God knows how they expect anybody to fight on that shit, you couldn't even fuck on it!'

Tinleg laughed hollowly, his open mouth filled with a mixture of insect and porridge. 'That's a good one, Teeth. Neither of us has had a woman these three years. We wouldn't know which end to start at any more. Besides,' he added, bolting down another greedy spoonful, 'the way things are now, there ain't goin' to be much likelihood that we're ever goin' to rip one off in the future. Our future's down there, brother.' He pointed to the earth floor of the bunker. 'Watching the sunflowers grow from two metres below.'

Teeth didn't speak for a moment. In the next bunker, the soldier whose both legs had been shot away and still lived although he was leaking blood by the bucketful moaned piteously. 'Croak him,' a hoarse voice protested, 'croak the noisy bastard! I can't get my head down for the shitting noise.'

Vulf dropped into the hole in a shower of dirt, bottle gripped in his hand, for he seemed to have an uncanny talent for obtaining vodka anywhere.

'Well?' Teeth demanded, new urgency in his voice. 'What gives?'

Vulf took a deep swig of the fiery white spirit before he replied, 'Nothing gives.'

'What do you mean, you four-eyed craparse?' Tinleg asked a little angrily, finishing off the rest of the *Kavka*.

'I shall explain in simple terms, easily understandable by four-year-olds — and corporals in Punishment Battalion 333,' Vulf added pointedly. 'Our dear colonel is going to stick it out. He will not abandon Krasnaya.'

'May his wife's tits and belly torment him to his dying day!' Tinleg exploded. 'Doesn't he know we don't stand a chance in hell here?'

Vulf finished the last of the vodka and tossed the empty bottle on to the earth floor carelessly. 'He might well know, Corporal, but he's not admitting it to anyone — not even himself, our Colonel Katukov. No, not even to himself...'

The December day passed with leaden feet. There was little military activity from either German position, save for the routine burst of machine-gun fire and, at regular intervals, mortar-fire, but the regular hollow boom of metal on metal beyond the hills on the other side indicated that the German engineers were already preparing the sections of the pontoon bridge for the night-time operation; and just after midday when the sun vanished and the sky hazed over with snow clouds, a fresh arrow of red flares was lit in the positions occupied by the glider-borne troops.

The Marshal lowered his binoculars gloomily and looked at Livny. The other answered his unspoken question with a slight nod. 'Yes, it is one of the penalties of being clever. One asks the right questions and gets the wrong answers.' He attempted to smile at his humour and failed badly. 'They're expecting further landings.' The Marshal looked at his watch. There were about three hours until darkness now. Three hours to think out a plan of escape and execute it.

'The snow,' Livny said, as if able to read his mind. 'We'll have a regular old storm within the hour. It would be just the cover we needed, if —' He left the rest of his sentence unsaid, but the Marshal knew what he meant.

'Try to convince that damned colonel that,' he said bitterly. 'But surely now with the signal beacon,' Livny began, but the other man cut him short.

'No, he won't! The Katukovs of this world are rigid, set-mind men. Once they have made their decision, it takes a damned earthquake to make them change it. Reinforcements or not, he will keep us here.'□

Livny nodded gloomily and relapsed into a morose silence as the wind outside started to freshen, lifting up little swirls of dancing snow from the steppe and making the firs in the forest behind their position creak and bend.

'What if we *made* him withdraw while there was still time? We'd save the Battalion that way, even if we were forcing him against his will.'

The Marshal shook his head. 'Mutiny,' he grunted laconically, 'and he'd make every single one of us pay for it when and if we made it back.'

Livny said, 'Yes, I suppose you're right. We'd save his life and he'd still insist on our being arrested by those green-cross bastards of the NKVD. But there must be a way, Boldin, whether he likes it or not. There *must!*'

Boldin did not answer. He had no solution either.

Again time passed slowly. Each officer slumped there preoccupied with his own gloomy thoughts, while outside the hammering from the other bank continued, muted every now and again by the sudden shriek of the ever-increasing wind, already bearing with it the first hesitant flakes of the new snow.

'The only way to make Katukov move back,' Livny said slowly, finally breaking the heavy silence of the dug-out, 'is to take him to the rear on all fours.'

'What do you mean?'

'Well, Boldin, if he were wounded or hurt, say unconscious, he would have no say in the matter. Whether he liked it or not, he would have to be evacuated.'

'Agreed, but you're forgetting one thing, my *very* intelligent friend,' Boldin said a little cynically, 'Our dear colonel is neither wounded nor unconscious, and by the time that very distinct possibility takes place, we — all of us — will have joined him, making presumably very handsome stiffs.'

'Yes, Boldin,' Livny hesitated only very slightly, looking around to check if anyone might be listening to their conversation. 'But let us say that we helped the Fritzes in the matter?'

'What the hell are you talking about, Livny?' the Marshal exploded, exasperated by their situation, Katukov, Livny's mysterious statement, the whole damned war.

'This…'

CHAPTER 7

The snow foamed and whirled through the half-veiled trees, slashing across the canal, urged to every new fury by the frenzied shrieking wind. Visibility was down to twenty metres and soon, when the daylight finally went, the watching men knew it would be zero.

The Marshal hesitated no longer. It was now or never. He raised his hand. Stiffly the other three, their shoulders already heavy with snow, got to their feet.

The snow pounded against their faces and worked its way into their nostrils, ears and eyes, poking into them with icy numbing fingers. But they seemed not to notice it. Their narrowed-eyed gaze was fixed on the snow-covered command bunker and the stark outline of the freezing sentry posted at its entrance, his shoulders and head bowed miserably against the whirling snowflakes. 'Piotr the pimp,' Teeth whispered to the Marshal.

'*Horoscho*,' the Marshal hissed back. 'Pimps have their uses, but this day, I think we can do without him.'

'Crazy,' Tinleg whispered, 'absolutely crazy. Having to attack your own commander like this.'

'Hold yer water,' Teeth threatened, 'or you'll have my attack boot up yer skinny little crippled arse. All right, ready to go, Comrade Major.'

The Marshal flung a look around him. Nothing was to be seen in the howling snowstorm; they could not have wished for better cover. 'Go!' he called.

Behind him, Livny called in German, '*Sturmangriff*... *Sturmangriff*!' as Teeth pelted forward, showing surprising speed for such a big man.

Piotr the Pimp swung round, fumbling with his rifle sling. Too late. Teeth's hand grabbed the back of his helmet and pulled hard. The chin-strap slipped down his neck. The Pimp's face turned brick red. His eyes rolled upwards and his knees sagged beneath him. He was unconscious. Teeth lowered him to the ground, saying, 'Sleep tight, my little one.'

Now the rest of them doubled forward through the flying snow, making as much noise as they could, Livny crying out in German, simulating the attack which was the cover for what they were about to do.

The Marshal reached the dug out's entrance first. He yanked the pin out of the bomb and flung it into the darkness below, from which came the colonel's angry demands for information. It exploded at once, with streams of blinding white smoke coming from it. An instant later the blinded Katukov came staggering up to the surface, hands held out in front of him, feeling the way as best he could.

Teeth flashed an appealing look at the Marshal.

The Marshal nodded urgently, while at his side the one-eyed captain cried in German, 'Kill the dog!'

Teeth sighed and then drew back his fist. With all his strength he smashed it into the face of the blinded officer. Katukov smashed against the sandbagged wall, hung there groggily for a moment, while the rest watched him, their faces a mixture of awe and horror. Then his legs gave way and slowly he sank to the snowy ground. 'God in heaven,' Teeth moaned, as he bent down to pick up the unconscious officer, 'they'll have the nuts off of me with a blunt razorblade for this, if they ever find out!'

Vulf peered through the blinding snow and shook his head in admiration, realizing immediately what the little bunch of Gulag rats were about: now they had their pretext for evacuating the Krasnaya position. The Fritzes had attacked and the Colonel had been "wounded". Overwhelmed by superior enemy forces, they had been forced to withdraw, with or without the colonel's permission. If that hard bastard Boldin managed to get what was left of Punishment Battalion 333 back to their own lines safely, the plotters might just get away with it. If not, the Fritzes or a firing squad of the NKVD would solve all their problems — *permanently*. Vulf sniffed. All the same, the truth about what had really happened at Krasnaya this day might be useful sometime in the future, if they made it back. *If...*

The snow fell from the sky almost vertically and then a moment later when the wind caught it, was piled in drifts against the firs and driven into the faces of the tense, anxious men waiting for the order to move out.

The Marshal, at the head of the column, turned. Narrowing his eyes to slits against the storm, he stared back at his men, their heads buried miserably in the shelter of their greatcoat collars. They looked about at the end of their tether, and in the middle of the column they were burdened by nearly twenty stretcher cases. It was going to be a risky business, making their way along the canal bank for nearly three hundred metres before breaking out into no-man's-land, where for all they knew they stood a good chance of bumping into marauding German airborne troops. But the risk had to be taken and they did have the advantage of the howling storm on their side; it would make the Fritzes keep their heads down. 'All right, Sergeant-major,' he ordered Teeth, 'pass it on. Move out!'

'Move out!' the command flew from mouth to mouth. The men straightened up and clutched their weapons in hands which were wet with sweat in spite of that terrible cold. The bearers took the strain of the stretcher-cases.

'March or croak,' the Marshal said grimly, as he strode forward, tommy gun at the ready.

'March or croak ... *march or croak*!' The phrase went the length of the column. It was like the last prayer of some condemned criminal. 'MARCH OR CROAK...'

The Marshal spotted the Fritz sentry just in time: a stark black silhouette outlined momentarily against the flying white snowflakes.

'Teeth!' he hissed.

The big NCO needed no instructions. He darted forward, body crouched low. The Fascist never knew what hit him. Teeth reached up and pulled hard. The sentry's helmet slid backwards. Teeth thrust his right knee into the small of the man's back and pulled with all his great strength. Writhing frantically, weaving back and forth, the German fought to break that killing pressure on his throat. To no avail. The Fritz was garrotted to death, with the chin-strap biting ever deeper into his throat until it had disappeared for good into the flesh and he was a limp hunk of dead meat in Teeth's grasp. Almost gently he lowered him to the ground and whispered, 'All clear, Comrade Major.'

The Marshal breathed a sigh of relief. Now they were clear of the Fritz bridgehead on their side of the canal. In front of them lay at least two or three kilometres of no-man's-land before they reached the Russian second line of defence. What lay out there, he didn't know or care. The main thing was to get through it quickly before the Fritzes became aware that the birds had flown and sent out patrols to intercept them.

He threw a quick glance at the green-glowing dial of his watch. One minute to go. While his men crouched on their haunches resting and the stretcher-bearers flung themselves exhausted into the snow, he counted off the seconds. '*Fifty-one, fifty-two ... fifty-nine, sixty!*' Dead on the minute the ammunition they had abandoned at their old positions exploded with a great roar that seemed to go on for ever and the sky to their rear suddenly split apart in an angry violet flame. Almost immediately the nervous Fritzes reacted, just as the Marshal hoped they would. Tracer started to zip through the white flying gloom and flares hissed into the sky, as the Fritzes prepared to meet the suicidal Russian counter-attack. The Marshal laughed at the success of his last trick. That should keep them occupied for a little while. Then his smile vanished as quickly as it had come.

'On your feet everywhere;' he snarled. 'Come on, get the lead out of those lazy butts of yours! Move it!'

There were grumbles and complaints everywhere, especially from the already exhausted stretcher-bearers. But the Marshal knew he could have no mercy this night, if he were going to rescue what was left of the Gulag rats. His big snow-encrusted boot thudded into the skinny ribs of one of the bearers carrying the still unconscious colonel. 'Come on, you lazy swine!' he commanded, 'get some pepper in your idle breeches. *Move!*'

He moved.

It was a strange, almost unbearably long night, full of sudden frights and alarms. Twice they were fired upon by unseen men on the right flank, caught unprepared by angry bursts of tracer;

whether from their own patrols or marauding Fritzes, they did not stop to find out, but disappeared into the whirling snow without even returning the fire.

Once, too, they ran into what had obviously been well-prepared positions, and although they were no longer defended, it took them a nerve-racking, anxious hour to get through them in the darkness, fighting the half-buried barbed wire and the concealed pits, burdened as they were with the wounded. The wind increased to gale force, howling and whipping up the snow to a frenzy so that they seemed to be fighting a solid wall of flying flakes, making every step forward a minor achievement.

They began to file through a ravine, which acted as a natural tunnel for the snow storm. Now it was virtually impossible to keep one's eyes open for more than a couple of seconds and when they did the snow seemed to be coming at them like flak and hitting their crimson, streaming faces with the same impact.

Now the trail behind them started to become littered with abandoned equipment, as the exhausted Gulag rats began to throw away anything — everything — which impeded their snail-like progress. It was stained too with the blood-faeces squeezed from bodies already emaciated to mere skin and bones.

Men attempted to drop out. NCOs such as Teeth grabbed their weapons and forced the wildly staggering soldiers to continue. Twice the Marshal had to threaten to shoot an exhausted man, lying weeping piteously in the snow, if he did not get up and march: and twice his threat worked.

The hours passed with murderous slowness. They stumbled on slowly, all attempt at caution abandoned now, hanging on to the greatcoat of the man in front, kept on their feet solely by the desire to escape from the German trap and the Marshal's tough, inspired leadership; for in spite of his own weariness, he was here, there and everywhere along the column, threatening, cajoling, encouraging, at times burdening himself with two or three rifles taken from men too weary to carry the weapons themselves.

Dawn came reluctantly. They marched on through that vast empty landscape like black insignificant ants against the blinding white snow, as if God had abandoned them and the world, sick of its inhumanity and mindless cruelty.

The very steppe breathed hostility. It stretched to the horizon, awesome and brooding, littered here and there with burnt-out trucks and tanks, dotted by wrecked, abandoned villages in which the very crumbs had been picked off the kitchen floors by their starving predecessors who had fled this way.

Once they came across a ghastly tableau of dead bodies heaped indiscriminately together, their nationality indeterminate, the surface of the new snow broken only by waxen, iron-hard frozen arms. The Marshal ordered the exhausted men to halt there while he took his bearings. But the dead men offered no aid and in the end he had to confess to a worried Livny that he did not know where he was and where their own lines were. They stumbled on, staggered wildly from side to side, their exhausted faces an ashen green, their pain-racked bodies mechanically carrying them forward by a sheer effort of naked willpower, forced on by the blind unreasoning fear that somewhere out there in that white wilderness there was the enemy.

By ten that morning, with the only sound the gasp of their own breath as it escaped from their lungs in harsh hectic wheezes, the Marshal started to tell himself that they had successfully escaped from the Fritzes. But that wasn't to be, altogether.

Just as they emerged from the snow-heavy fir forest through which they had been trudging, sometimes up to their knees in fresh snow, a heavy-set figure suddenly barred their way.

The Marshal stopped dead and for what seemed an age the two men faced each other, neither knowing from the nondescript uniform each wore whether the man opposite was an enemy or not.

It was the one stranger who spoke first. It was his own undoing, for his challenge was in German!

The Marshal jerked up his submachine-gun. Violently it erupted at his side. A vicious stream of slugs struck the German at close range, whirling him round and round in a terrible, grotesque dance of death.

Bone splintered audibly. His blood splattered the snow in ugly red gobs, and as his scream of absolute, long-drawn-out agony reached its crescendo, his bullet-ridden body was slammed helplessly against the trunk of the nearest fir. He slipped down it and sat there, surrounded by an ever-growing circle of his own blood, head flopped to one side, dead.

The Marshal, followed by Teeth, floundered through the deep snow to where he sat, weapons at the ready, but the dead German was alone. Slowly they lowered their weapons and stared down at him, his face blank of any emotion, green eyes staring sightlessly at the unfeeling sky. Where he had come from and what he was doing there alone, seemingly kilometres away from his own people, they never learned, nor did they have time to consider the mystery, for were they not hunted men with the victorious Fritzes at their heels? So what was left of Punishment Battalion 333 commenced the laborious progress eastwards again, leaving behind a trail of their own blood, not knowing that that mysterious lone dead German, who had appeared so abruptly from nowhere, would be the one who got closest to Moscow in the whole four years of the terrible war in the East. One hour later the frightened young voice which challenged them from the frozen bushes with a high-pitched 'Stoi' told them they had reached their own lines at last. They were saved…

BOOK FOUR: *DECISION AT MOSCOW*

'I'm not going to appeal to your patriotism —
Mother Russia in danger and that shit!... I'm
appealing to your self-interest and instinct for
self-preservation.'
Vulf to the Gulag Rats, December 1941.

CHAPTER 1

Now Moscow was starving; there was just no relief from hunger. Under their shabby coats, the bellies of the Muscovites were distended by malnutrition or their flesh hung from their bones in raddled dewlaps. Their eyes were too large and glowing in their grey shrunken faces with long yellow fangs that fell away easily from shrunken gums, riddled with scurvy-ulcers.

Now the war and food became the civilians' main concern. Dogs and "roof hares" (cats) were hunted down remorselessly, and the flesh eaten raw in some cases or charred in the smouldering embers of bomb-shattered buildings.

Search parties of old women and children were organized to scavenge for anything edible. Every railway truck, warehouse, and bombed shop was searched for food. The dust from the wooden floors of flour mills was swept up as if it were from gold, and bagged. Flour sacks were carefully beaten to the same end. Sheep gut, lubricant, fishmeal meant for farmers were mixed and turned into sausage. Soap was turned into jelly. When one of the few remaining skinny-ribbed nags collapsed of starvation in the streets, police rushed to guard it with drawn pistols until it could be dragged off to the factory, again under armed guard, to be turned into the inevitable sausage. Sheep intestines, mixed with cloves, became milk. Even wallpaper was stripped from the walls so that the size and dried flour which had been used to glue it up could be turned into dough for baking bread.

In spite of the desperate, never-ending search for food that December, the citizens of the capital had to subordinate their entire lives to the interests of the front.

Although most of the great factories had already been evacuated on Stalin's orders, the Muscovites were forced in some cases, or encouraged in orders, to undertake the production of mortars, rocket-guns, cannon, and rifles, to be rushed to the front which was now less than twenty kilometres away. For now everyone knew that it was only "General Winter" who could hold the Fritzes at bay until new divisions were formed within the capital itself to beat the temporarily stalled Germans. As the bold red slogan everywhere proclaimed: '*The defeat of Germany must begin in front of Moscow!*'

And still the wounded poured in from the front. Hospitals overflowed into schools and schools into warehouses — there simply wasn't enough accommodation to hold the thousands upon thousands of soldiers being unloaded from the trains and ambulances by the hour. Nearly one third of the survivors of Punishment Battalion 333 landed in one such temporary hospital four days after they were challenged by that frightened young sentry.

First they were stripped naked, and lying on the floor of what had once obviously (to judge by the parallel bars on the walls) been a school gymnasium, they were deloused, their skinny naked bodies, here and there disfigured by huge gaping wounds, being sprayed by a white powder which sent the lice fleeing for cover by their thousands. Then the ice-cold showers in the roof were turned on; there was no fuel available for hot water, in spite of temperatures which were well below freezing.

Then the "treatment", if it could be called that, commenced. Only the most serious cases warranted drugs. Their wounds were cleaned by surgeons, whose rubber aprons and boots were splashed with dried blood, while the agony-racked wounded bit their lips until they were bloody or, if they were in luck, took deep swallows from litre bottles of vodka. Then they were dressed with paper bandages and the men put two or even three in a bed.

The Marshal's frost-bitten feet were not even treated by a doctor, but by a cross-eyed, evil-smelling orderly, who pulled off the officer's boots with one agonizing tug after the other, and then proceeded to strip off Boldin's socks, while the Marshal, his brow wreathed in sweat, twisted in sheer agony.

The socks were full of big patches of skin, where his toes were all white blisters, but his heels were the worst. The flesh was red-raw, though not a drop of blood came from it.

The orderly bent his head to them and took a deep breath.

'Attar of roses?' the Marshal ventured through gritted teeth. Irony was wasted on the man. 'Gone soft and stinky,' he said. 'Bad frostbite.' He began to pull off the remaining skin with his dirty fingernails.

That was his "treatment" for the first day. On the second, when the bulk of the Punishment Battalion's casualties had been attended to, a young under-lieutenant doctor came to visit him. Without much ado, he dug his forceps into the sole of the Marshal's right foot. 'Can you feel anything, Major?' he asked.

'A bit,' Boldin answered warily.

'Might be able to save your feet if we're lucky,' the young doctor said casually. Thus the Marshal learnt he had third-degree frostbite.

But the treatment, painful as it was, had its compensations.

They came in the shape of Sister 1st Class Lydia Pechenka, extremely blonde, highly efficient and very beautiful.

The Marshal, exhausted as he was from the front and the treatment, had a sleepless night. For hours, while the German bombers droned overhead monotonously, his head whirled and he couldn't get to sleep: Sister 1st Class Lydia Pechenka, who could have been his daughter, would not leave his mind, however much he rationalized about her attraction for an "old man" like himself.

Two days went by without her seeming to notice him; her gaze always concentrated on his red-raw feet, while she deftly painted them with some healing solution and made the usual quick notation on the graph at the foot of his bed. Then the colonel of anti-aircraft artillery, who had been wounded by a shell driving-ring falling from one of his own cannon and shared the little ward with him, commented very loudly so that the whole corridor packed with wounded men outside could hear: 'I'd give a couple of copecks to get up her lace drawers any day!' And he had laughed coarsely and made an explicit gesture with a clasped thumb and forefinger of one hand.

In spite of the pain in his feet, the Marshal had been out of his own cot in a flash and the surprised artilleryman had reeled back, clutching a suddenly bleeding nose.

That day Lydia looked at him and smiled when she treated his frost-bitten feet and when she left to attend to other patients she presented him with two very precious slabs of milk chocolate. The Marshal was happier than he had been for many a year. His feet started to improve rapidly.

While the wounded recovered in the makeshift hospital and Colonel Katukov was absent outside the beleaguered capital, recruiting new cannon-fodder for his command, the survivors were employed in acting as rescue and burial parties after the daily German air-raid.

Red Cross sisters took care of the rescued; it was the dead who were the problem, for as soon as the all-clear sirens commenced their unholy wail the looters swarmed out of the still smoking ruins like the rats they were to plunder the corpses.

More than once Teeth and Tinleg in charge of a party of Gulag rats, their faces covered by gas-masks to keep out the stench of death, came across looters, often women, searching the dead with vulture-like avidness and swift efficient routine, sometimes slicing off fingers in order to get at rings. Then, without even a word of warning, Teeth's submachine-gun would chatter and later Tinleg would hobble from looter to looter as he or she lay writhing on the bloodstained cobbles and blow the backs of their heads off.

The dead they buried in open graves, heaving in the corpses from the city's refuse-carts, covering each layer of bodies with lime before starting a new one so that in the end the mass grave looked like one of those turnip "pies" in which the *kolhoz* farmer stored his turnips and potatoes over the winter.

It was terrible work, the dead sometimes coming apart in their hands as they pulled them out of the rubble, and they were drunk all the time, even taking the filters out of their gas-masks and replacing them with rags soaked in vodka so that the fumes drove out the sickly cloying stench of the dead.

For identification purposes it had been ordered that bodies found in the same shelter or cellar should be kept together, and more than once the Gulag rats, nauseated and vomiting all the while, were forced to pour the thick, congealed, black goo which had once been human beings into a horse-trough or tin bath-tub and carry the dead thus to the nearest mass grave, with on top a note of how many dead there were in the container. On one occasion they managed to get fifty phosphorus bomb victims into such a bath-tub and were drunk for twenty-four hours solid afterwards. It was the only way that they could keep sane.

But in spite of the starvation, bombing, the terrible conditions that December in Moscow and the apparently deserted ruined streets, there was a hectic clandestine night life in the capital, if one knew where to look for it, and Teeth and Tinleg needed no seeing-eyed guide-dogs to help them find what they sought — *women*!

The two of them disdained the official Red Army brothels, graded into three classes (officers, NCOs, and soldiers) in spite of the fact that they existed in a supposed "classless society", where a NKVD guarded the entrance and a medical orderly gave the would be pleasure-seeker a medical examination before he was allowed to join the line of waiting soldiers, each armed with a five-rouble note in one hand and a contraceptive plus a log of wood to heat the place in the other.

Night after night after they were finished, they would stagger drunkenly through the ruined streets, above them the icy fingers of the searchlights parting the clouds looking for the Fritz bombers and the flak pounding away, dodging the NKVD patrols or hitting them hard and running for their lives if they couldn't, chanting that drunken doggerel of theirs, 'Vodka … vodka a mattress polka with a big-titted wench and a slug in the skull to make a happy stiff … vodka … vodka…' Over and over again until the thrumming of a balalaika and the muted laughter of women from some cellar or other told them they had found what they sought — women.

Then they would fling open the door to the screams and shouts of the women and men below in the candlelit, smoke-filled underground room, crying, 'The Gulag rats are here, wenches! Knickers off and legs apart, it's been a long time since yesterday!' And when the other men in the cellar objected, Teeth's ham like fist and occasionally Tinleg's wicked little knife soon convinced them that the 'Gulag rats' were indeed welcome, even honoured guests.

The whores, amateur and professional, loved the two NCOs. In a city where the old men or Party officials who had the food to buy women were often impotent and the young men, who weren't, had no food, the two tough virile Gulag rats were men who could do no wrong. Staggering into the candlelit centre of some warm cellar, heavy with the fug of many cigarettes, male sweat, cheap powder and the pot-bellied glowing metal stove in the corner, they would start taking off their uniforms even before they had deigned to select the whore for the night, crying to the delight of the giggling women, 'Rip off the rags, ladies, we're gonna dance a wonderful mattress-polka this night, my beloveds!'

And surprisingly enough the hard-bitten whores with their raddled, berouged faces, deep circles under their eyes, would respond with alacrity like virginal brides on their first night; and Teeth would sigh happily to his running-mate as they succumbed to the willing whores, 'Tinleg, you little cripple, don't ever wake me up again. Let me die here — *on the job*!'

But unknown to the survivors of the Punishment Battalion, while they enjoyed their time out of war, death was not far away again.

Colonel Katukov, his nose still swollen and mottled green from that terrible punch that Teeth had "planted" upon him, was already busy recruiting new "Gulag rats" to fill out the gaps in his decimated Battalion. Day after day, accompanied only by his clerk Vulf, he toured the camps of the Moscow District area, seeking recruits, who were ever more difficult to find, now that the word of the terrible defeats suffered by the Red Army had arrived there.

He allowed himself no respite. Despite the deep snow and roads and tracks, often blocked two metres high with snow and ice, he forced a crippling pace on Vulf, who drove skidding from side on side on the slippery surface, one hand on the wheel, the other on his precious bottle of pepper vodka, his only solace in this terrible frozen world of desolation and misery. At the camps, he was met by mute emaciated faces. The "Gulag rats" could not be tempted to join either by appeals to their patriotism or the fact that they would be freed immediately and their sentences be cancelled: in that grim month of December 1941, the chances of survival seemed greater in the Gulag than at the front.

In the end it was Vulf who found the recruits that the colonel required. 'Let me have a go, Colonel,' he pleaded after another disappointing day at the camps, where they had succeeded in enlisting four new recruits and one of them was a simpleton who appeared to think he was joining some sort of religious order that would 'clear the Godless out of our Holy Russia!'

'I speak their language, you don't.'

'What do you mean, Vulf?' Katukov asked wearily.

'Give me a free hand and I'll show you,' Vulf replied with a grin and a mocking look in those cunning eyes of his.

'All right, *anything*, but get me bodies.'

'Bodies, you shall have, Colonel, but don't ask too many questions about them,' Vulf said softly and Katukov affected not to hear, wisely as it turned out later.

The next morning with a hard blue winter sky outlining the camp in all its stark bleak misery and the crows cawing hoarsely in the skeletal frozen branches of the naked trees,

Vulf addressed the assembled prisoners, while Katukov watched him from the commandant's office.

In spite of his shabby intellectual appearance and the horn-rimmed glasses which marked him as a professor, Vulf had a certain kind of presence, Katukov had to admit reluctantly. Even the prisoners were curious, perhaps even impressed by this weedy figure standing in front of them in an ill-fitting, shabby private's uniform, the front of his blouse stained with food, snuff and vodka he had spilled down it.

Vulf took his time. He allowed them the farts, the coarse sniggers that followed, the hoarse whispers about his appearance, his parentage and the like, and waited till the freezing cold had them stamping their feet and clapping their arms to and fro across their skinny chests; then he began.

'Comrades, as you are well aware, you are the scum of the earth!' He said the words baldly, without emotion, accusation, irony, anything.

They had their effect, especially as he added a moment later with perfect timing, 'Or so the Party bosses and the NKVD tell us.'

There were hoarse laughs on all sides and Vulf knew instinctively he had won these half-starved scarecrows, who shivered in the icy wind like aspen leaves.

'But scum of the earth as you are, you have survived so far when many a party commissar is already looking at the turnips from beneath out there to the west or has had his eggs tickled off him by some nasty Fritz with a blunt razorblade!'

The Gulag rats laughed, hardly believing their own ears that someone could talk about the hated, feared NKVD like that in the middle of a Gulag camp.

Vulf's face hardened. 'Naturally you think that you are safer here in the camp than at the front. So far that has been the case. But once the Fritzes break through the Moscow front, which they certainly will do if we don't find reinforcements, things will be different.'

'Why?' a bold voice called from the rear rank, 'we hate those Red bastards in Moscow, they do, too. Why should they harm us?'

The sudden question did not worry Vulf. 'The Ukrainians thought the same as you in the summer when the Fritzes first marched in. The headmen welcomed the Fritzes with bread and salt in each village they marched into. They thought the Fritzes had come to liberate them. And what happened, comrades? I'll tell you. Within the month the Gestapo were stringing up Ukrainians from telegraph masts from Kiev to Brest-Litovsk. End of the Ukrainian independence movement. No, comrades.' Vulf's voice rose. 'When the Fritzes come, it won't mean liberation for you Gulag rats, it'll mean a quicker death, because the Gestapo is more efficient than the NKVD.' He laughed.

No one joined him. Their skinny faces remained sombre and suddenly thoughtful, as if many of them had thought the Germans might well come as liberators not murderers.

Vulf pressed home his point. 'I'm not going to appeal to your patriotism — Mother Russia in danger and all that shit! No, not one bit. What I'm appealing to is your self-interest and instinct for self-preservation.'

'What do you mean?' someone asked hoarsely.

'This. You volunteer to get out of the camps to be freed of your sentences and get some bacon under yer skinny ribs. But it doesn't mean that you've got to go and have yer stupid turnips blown off at the front in short order. Not one bit of it.'

He lowered his voice and with the trick of a professional lecturer, their interest caught now, had them craning their heads forward to catch his next words. 'There is a long road between here and the front. Men can get lost, if you follow me?' He winked solemnly.

They followed him well enough and waited for more.

'Even if a skilled man can't get lost, and I would have thought that a Gulag rat who can't do that doesn't deserve much better than a Fritz slug through his heart, the front has its compensations.' Vulf looked directly at the skinny runt of a cross-eyed ex-pimp and whore-master in the centre of the front rank of prisoners. 'There's women and loot and black market pickings everywhere. A wise man could make himself a tidy fortune in gold up there and there's always some fool of a peasant boy, straight from the farm with the hay still piled up behind his dirty ears, who'll go and do your fighting for you — at a small price. For a bigger one, he'll go and get his *kolhoz* turnip blow off for you, too!'

This time the men laughed. The crooks among them, already imagining how they could milk the front before disappearing into the nearest big city, taking a dive and living off their earnings until the war was over and they could start up business once more, started to suck their front teeth thoughtfully.

Vulf pressed home his attack. 'We're not taking everybody,' he said, raising his voice now. 'The first four hundred to put up their hands will have the first chance of being selected by Colonel Katukov, the next —'

The rest of his words were drowned in the clamour of half a thousand voices, with hands shooting up everywhere. '*Me ... me*,' they yelled, jostling and shoving each other in their eagerness to be considered for the honour of joining Punishment Battalion 333.

That night the first convoy of new replacements for Katukov's battalion started to crawl through the night towards Moscow and Vulf assured a stern-faced Katukov drunkenly, 'Give me another week, Comrade Colonel, and I'll raise you a whole damned division…'

CHAPTER 2

But Vulf was not fated to have that additional week, for already things were beginning to move in the capital, as the *Stavka* and Stalin finalized their plans for the great counter-offensive now that the weather was beginning to settle again and the Germans could be expected to attack once more. If they didn't beat them, the Marshals knew, the Fritzes would overrun the capital and then Russia would collapse.

The Marshal, hobbling around clumsily now in thick felt socks, first became aware of the impending change when Lydia waited till the artillery Colonel had departed for his morning sojourn in the officers' latrine, complete with *Pravda* which hid the pornographic magazine he was addicted to and the *Trud* under his arm, and then spoke in a hurried whisper: 'A commission arrives tomorrow.'

'A commission!'

'Yes, to grade the wounded. They always do that when they need men for the front, Comrade Major.' Her bottom lip trembled and the Marshal thought he caught a suspicion of a tear in her beautiful eyes.

With unaccustomed tenderness for him, he patted her hand with his sabre-scarred paw. 'Come, Lydia, it is not so tragic. Soldiers come, soldiers go. You must be sick of seeing them and the misery they bring with them.'

'It isn't misery.' Her voice broke off and she could say no more.

That night they became lovers. In her cellar room beneath the temporary hospital, with the dirty walls heaving and trembling under the impact of the German bombs, he took her fiercely, almost brutally. She responded with the same fire. With the ruined city outside forgotten while the candle flickered wildly, magnifying their shadows gigantically, grotesquely, they allowed their frenzied desire to consume them, as if there had never been another lovemaking like it. Outside the world went mad.

Later she cried. But not for the reason he supposed. Dabbing her tears away, she whispered, 'The front ... is it terrible?'

'Don't talk about it,' he urged, watching her beautiful face, now stained by tears, one lock of lovely blonde hair hanging over her forehead. 'It is not important.'

'But it is! Why can't it leave us alone? It consumes everything and what it leaves is ruined. Don't you think I know? I see them every day and however much you may pretend to yourself that they are just cases — stomach cases, lung cases, leg cases — they are tortured human beings.'

He patted her hand to comfort her. 'I know ... I know. Death in action is better. It's clean and it's final. It's the business of being wounded that —' He broke off suddenly, while the cellar shook violently under the impact of yet another HE bomb.

'Must you go?' she asked in a little voice. 'After all *they* have done to you, why should you fight for them? You've done enough as it is.'

He did not answer immediately, as if he were seriously considering what she just had said; then he shook his head. 'Gulag rat I may be Lydia, but I am a Russian. I must go when they call me.' His voice strengthened. 'It's my duty to my country.'

'Then you will see me no more,' she said, tugging her bodice closed.

'I will see you no more,' he echoed.

Outside with the sky over the Kremlin glowing fiercely, the two of them, strangely uneasy and apart now, almost bumped into the ancient crone staring at the heavens. She laughed, revealing a toothless mouth, and croaked, using the peasant phrase, 'The angels are baking bread up there this night, ain't they?'

'No,' Lydia snapped, her voice hard and unyielding, 'not the angels, *but devils...*'

Stalin did not see that burning sky, in which the "angels" baked their bread. At that particular moment he and his Marshal were in deep cellars beneath the Kremlin, which, so his experts maintained, could stand a direct hit by the largest bomb known to be employed by the Fritzes; he had other things on his mind than peasant sayings.

He had come a long way since those days when as a barefoot peasant boy he had made his dusty, shy way to the seminary in his Georgian homeland where he was to learn to be a Greek Orthodox *pope*. He had been a bank robber, a revolutionary, a terrorist, a party functionary; slowly working his way upwards within the Party with that cunning ruthless persistence of his until finally he had succeeded the great Lenin himself.

Now that whole position of power which had taken him so long to build up was threatened by that fool Hitler, or "Gitler", as he pronounced the name when he spoke to his cronies of the German dictator. Why had he ever trusted the man? Why had he not listened to Churchill, drunken sot that he was, when he had warned him that the Germans were going to attack Russia? Then he had thought Churchill's warning a provocation to drag him into the war which England was so patently losing; now he knew better.

Now while he brooded and his marshals waited in that dark sombre underground room, the only sound that of his own heavy breathing and the muted thud of the enemy bombs outside, time was running out for Russia. He knew it and the soldiers did too. Yet Stalin knew too that battles were often won not by numbers alone but by courage, resolve and boldness. Hadn't the Whites outnumbered them back in 1919-1920 and hadn't half the capitalist world aided the reactionaries? Still they had won, because they had never thought of the possibility of defeat; their sense of mission, purpose, had been too strong even to allow, mentally, of that eventuality. In their hearts they had known the Whites could not possibly win.

He looked at his marshals and knew his first battle would be with them, if he were to save Moscow and Russia. Some of them feared him, most of them hated him and it was fear and hate that kept them obeying his orders. But they wouldn't be capable of winning battles on that basis. They had lost fight after fight since the Germans had invaded Russia in the summer; now their confidence had to be restored, not by threats as in the past, but by new hope that success was at last within their reach if they would attempt to grasp it.

'Soldiers,' he said finally, 'my commanders.'

'They looked at him, their broad hard faces clearly revealing their astonishment at being addressed thus. For years Stalin had never attempted to hide his contempt of them; now he was addressing them as "my commanders".

Stalin forced a smile, giving them the benefit of that avuncular smile which had decorated the multi-coloured posters carried past the Kremlin by the *komsolu* before the war on Red Army Day. 'Napoleon said after the Battle of Borodino that he had not the troops for any more fighting, otherwise he would lose the advantages of the great victory he had just won.' He let the words sink in before adding, 'Hitler is in the same position. Let us be frank about it, my commanders, he *has* won a great victory on the Volga Canal. But has he the troops to exploit that victory?' Stalin answered his own question, knowing as he did so that he was lying; after all he had the figures. 'No, he hasn't, comrades. We in defeat, *have* the troops, however. We must now use them. Comrade Zhukov, your plan?'

Zhukov started. He had no plan. He was hanging on to Moscow by the skin of his teeth. Plans for offensive operations were furthest from his mind, yet the manner in which Stalin had spoken to him told him that for once the dictator would listen; he would not attempt to impose his will on his soldiers as he had done in the past, often with disastrous results. 'Plan,' he echoed, his brain racing, while the other marshals stared at him, eyes full of surprise and awe. Zhukov had a plan when everything was falling apart. What could it be?

The dimpled-chinned Marshal with the barrel-chest cleared his throat like some pompous Party official who had all the facts at his finger-tips. 'I have come to the conclusion,' he improvised wildly, 'that Hitler's generals made a fatal decision when they opted for wheels and not tracks.'

The others stared at him, as if he had suddenly gone crazy. Stalin hid his smile. He had guessed right. Zhukov would be able to rise to the challenge.

'What do I mean by that? This. With tracked vehicles he would have been able to make it to Moscow even in the weather conditions we have experienced recently. With wheels that objective is impossible, and his infantry relies on wheels. Hence if we can defeat his armour, his infantry is at our mercy.' He forced a grin, beaming at them with more confidence than he felt. 'At least the wheels will enable his infantry to run away more quickly, once we've got them on the run, comrades, eh?'

There were few unenthusiastic murmurs of agreement.

'Now where is the gross of his armour?' Deliberately, his heavy, highly polished boots making a hollow noise on the ancient wooden floor of the cellar, he strode to the big wall map and slapped it twice with his heavy, ex-cavalryman's paw. 'Here to the south and up in the north of Moscow — here! We will attack both positions.' There was an excited buzz of voices at the announcement. Even Stalin seemed startled. Zhukov waited impassively for the noise to die away, his arms crossed over his massive chest, his face giving nothing away.

Finally the noise died down and Zhukov spoke. 'Where are we going to get the armour from to attack and destroy the Fritz tanks, you ask? *Tankovi niet* is the word all our infantry commanders have been receiving from the *Stavka* this last month, I know. And there are no more tanks available save those coming from the capital's factories. No, comrades, we shall have to match brawn and courage, naked courage, against steel. It will be the Civil War all over again.'

Stalin looked at the burly Marshal sharply. 'What do you mean?' he demanded.

'The Molotov cocktail and a good strong arm, Comrade Stalin,' was Zhukov's sole reply.

Now the order started to go out: Shock Armies One, Fifty and Sixty-One, Stand By... Alert State One... Red Air Fleet Six, Max Effort... Partisan Groups Six and Ten, prepare for immediate anti-fascist operations... All that night they were sent, by radio, telephone, courier, dispatch-rider, telegram, order after order, until finally the individual units were mentioned, those which would provide those "strong arms". Immediate attention, all "Stalin Scholar" units and Punishment Battalions, hazardous mission proposal…

CHAPTER 3

'Now this is the drill,' Colonel Katukov cried to the assembled battalion, the pale emaciated faces of the new recruits from the Gulag standing out among the wind-reddened ones of the survivors, as they watched on the snowy barrack square. 'You rats probably think what I am going to do is highly dangerous, but it isn't. It is the kind of thing that some poor decent peasant boy has to do every day at the front.' He could not resist his normal sneer at the fighting ability of his Battalion.

The Marshal frowned, as the roar of the tank motors from the MT sheds to the right grew louder. Katukov could never let up. 'He probably wants us all dead before he'll admit that we might have a spark of courage in our cowardly bodies.' Livny whispered.

'Probably,' the Marshal agreed as the shell-scarred T-34, the only one they had been able to borrow in the whole of Moscow for this exercise, swung round the corner in a flurry of churned snow. Katukov crouched, in one hand the bottle of petrol, the wick already burning, in the other the limpet mine.

Now the T-34 started to advance upon him in low gear, moving at perhaps five kilometres an hour, the young driver obviously apprehensive of what was expected of him, especially as it was a full colonel of the NKVD who was going to carry out the operation.

'Faster!' Katukov bellowed above the roar of the T-34's motors. '*Faster, damn you!*'

Now he crouched there directly in the path of the thirty-ton tank. It came ever closer. *One hundred metres … fifty … thirty metres … twenty…*

At the very last moment, when it seemed that the tank must crush him to death, the big, hard-faced colonel acted. In the same instant he threw the burning bottle. It smashed against the low glacis plate of the tank, the liquid pouring down and momentarily blinding the driver, as Katukov anticipated it would. He hit the brakes hard and the T-34 swerved to one side. The colonel dashed forward with surprising speed and agility for such a big, wooden-faced man. Even before the gunner could swing the turret round and swat him off with the long overhanging cannon, as was the regulation drill in such a situation, he had pressed the limpet to the steel deck just above the motors with a great resounding clang and had dropped over the side.

'God in heaven,' Teeth breathed as the tank came to a halt and the colonel picked himself up from the snow, his chest heaving, but with a smile of triumph on his face, 'and that bastard wants us to do that! We might as well just let the Fritzes shoot us out in the open!'

'That you can say again, Teeth,' Tinleg agreed, his eyes wide with awe. 'Just me with my pegleg against thirty tons of armour. Old Leather Face must be out of his head to think that he's gonna knock out the Fascist tanks like *that*!'

But obviously the Soviet dictator and his underlings felt their plan to deal with the German armour in front of Moscow before the infantry went into the counterattack was a good one, for as Colonel Katukov summed up after he had caught his breath, 'It is very easy for even cowards like yourselves. The Molotov cocktail will set the glacis plate on fire temporarily and if nothing else upset the driver, as you saw in my case, and occupy the turret crew until it is too late for them to deal with the attacker. Then he's up on the back over the engine cowling and attaching his limpet. Thereafter nothing can detach it —

it's held there by powerful magnets.' He ventured a thin, wintry smile. 'Any flatfooted yokel from the country with the hayseed behind his ears could do it, just like that!'

He looked at the Marshal, who was asking himself at that particular moment what would happen if the machine-gunner of the following tank spotted the would-be tank destroyer or even if the tank in question was protected by supporting infantry, and snapped, 'Major, divide the Battalion into serials. This day every one of those rats is going to have a go!'

Boldin looked at him aghast. The new recruits were so weak for the most part that they could hardly hold their rifles; now they were expected to indulge in a manoeuvre that would tax a well-trained athlete. 'But Comrade Colonel —' he began.

'No buts, Major.' Katukov cut him short brutally. 'There is no time to be lost. *To work!*'

The Marshal turned glumly to Teeth. 'All right, Sergeant-major,' he commanded, 'sort them out into serials but for hell's sake, see that they can run and jump. Otherwise —' He left the rest of his sentence unsaid.

Teeth nodded. 'I understand, Comrade Major, 'he answered with unusual gravity for him and then added under his breath, 'I don't know, Marshal, but some of the brothers are going to be looking at the turnips from below this day, I'll warrant.'

The Marshal didn't reply; he couldn't.

All that morning the Gulag rats, divided into serials of two, practised the dangerous attack manoeuvre, with Teeth carefully selecting his best men first in the hope that Katukov would weary of the exercise and not return to the parade ground after the midday bowl of cabbage soup. He was mistaken; Katukov obviously wanted to see every man in his command have a go at the T-34.

At two that afternoon with the sky already beginning to cloud over as if fresh snow was on its way, Teeth himself partnered Tinleg, who stood in the path of the roaring tank while he ran at it to attach the limpet mine, with the colonel crying brutally, 'Run, damn you, Sergeant-major, *run!*'

He ran for all he was worth, the tracks whirling frighteningly at face level, showering him with snow, almost blinding him at times, as his big paws sought for some hold on the vehicle's armoured back. Just in time he avoided clutching the twin exhaust pipes, now a dull crimson with overheating, and instead pulled himself up and on the deck by a towing hook, knowing as he did so the exhaust would have burnt his flesh down to the bone. He clamped home his mine, dropped over the side and was promptly sick in the nearest ditch, while Katukov shouted through his megaphone, 'All right, come on, don't be all day about it — *the next one!*'

By three it was snowing hard and visibility was down to virtually zero; the flakes were coming down in a solid wall so that it was hard for the freezing Gulag rats to keep their eyes open more than a slit. But still Katukov persisted with the exercise, brushing aside the Marshal's protests with a brusque, 'Where wood is sawn, there is sawdust, Major. Casualties, if there are any, will teach those other rats of yours to be more on their toes in the future!'

Another half hour passed. Now most of the Battalion was through; all, indeed, save the officers.

The Marshal looked at Livny who was in his serial and shook his head even before the one-eyed captain spoke. 'No,' he said firmly, 'I shall place the limpet. I'm not a cripple, you know, Marshal. I can see better than most people who have two eyes.'

'No two ways about it, Livny, I'll take —'

'Captain Livny, you're the younger,' Katukov's voice broke into their discussion, 'you'll take the limpet.'

'Yes, Comrade Colonel,' Livny answered, throwing a triumphant glance at the Marshal.

The Marshal responded with a glum look but said nothing, as yet once again the tank driver revved up the T-34's 400 h.p. engines and then slammed home first gear.

Livny crouched, heavy limpet at the ready, the snow beating his face with great soft flakes so that he was forced to wipe it continually as the T-34 roared ever closer in low gear. To his right the Marshal waited too, Molotov cocktail raised, prepared to throw as soon as the tank was within range. All around them the others, their upper bodies coated in thick snow, tensed; they knew just how dangerous this was even for a man with both eyes.

'Now!' Katukov barked into his megaphone, the snow-laden wind catching his order and bearing it away immediately. But the Marshal heard the command. He grunted and hurled the bottle. It shattered right on the glacis plate and liquid, which in the real thing would already be a sea of oily flame, streamed down the armour. Livny didn't hesitate. He darted forward, limpet already raised to clamp home.

'Hurry it up,' Katukov urged through the megaphone. '*Hurry!*'

Now the rear of the tank was almost parallel with the one-eyed captain. He grabbed for a hold, momentarily blinded by the flying snow. In his haste he seized the red-hot right exhaust pipe.

He screamed with absolute agony, his right hand withering away in a flash. The air was suddenly full of the stench of burning flesh. Livny's feet went from under him. The track caught his flying boot. Suddenly he had vanished, being drawn under those flying vicious tracks, his scream drowned by the roar of motors. An instant later what was left of Captain Livny, arms, legs, head, indeterminate parts of the human body, was spread out in the bloody snow behind the suddenly stalled tank and the driver was vomiting out of the hatch, as if he would never be able to stop.

Katukov looked at the Marshal, the former's face a mixture of shock and perhaps a little fear of the other man's reaction.

The Marshal took his eyes off what was left of his friend, spread out over the ground, the snowflakes already beginning to bury him, as one day it would undoubtedly bury them all, the whole pack of them, the Gulag rats whose fate was to be sudden death, then he snarled, 'All right, you officers, don't just stand there who's next?'

The deadly training went on…

CHAPTER 4

Two days after the death of Captain Livny, Colonel Katukov again reinforced the impression he was making on the newly reformed Punishment Battalion 333. On the night of the accident some forty men of those talked into volunteering by Vulf's cunning decided that, perhaps, their services would be better employed elsewhere. Immediately after blackout that same night they had departed for the capital's centre, apparently preparing to make a "dive", find a whore, and live off her earnings, while they established themselves on the black market. They hadn't got far. The NKVD, which had thrown a cordon around all the barracks housing the men who would fight the counter-offensive, had arrested them by next morning. By the same evening the NKVD beatings had made them sing and now, beaten, bruised and hungry, they were returned to the Punishment Battalion to await their CO's decision about their futures.

Unlike most COs under such circumstances, who needed every man who could fire a rifle, Katukov was not prepared to let them off with pay and privileges all forfeited and the assignment to one of the most dangerous positions in an infantry unit at point or as scout. As he explained to the Marshal early that second morning, his face flushed with rage, his eyes blazing almost fanatically, 'The swine are not going to get away with it. I know I can't make them all pay the full price — I haven't got enough bodies as it is — but by the great whore of Kazan, I'm going to make an example of one in ten of them. Major, parade the Battalion!'

'What are you going to do, Comrade Colonel?' the Marshal asked in alarm. Ever since the training in the use of the limpet mine and Molotov cocktail, the men had been nervous and jumpy as it was; he didn't want them unsettled any further.

'Just parade the Battalion, Boldin, that's all. I'm expecting a visitor from the Lubyanka, he'll take care of this little bit of business once and for all.'

Thirty minutes later the Battalion had been paraded, the men shivered in their ankle-length greatcoats, stamping their feet in the frozen snow, their breath fogging the air in little grey clouds, while their officers eyed the huge furniture removal van with the Central Moscow number which had just driven into the barracks, wondering what role it would play in what was soon to come.

It was the appearance of Teeth and Tinleg directing a group of bent sweating fatigue men carrying a strange, wooden structure, which they started to erect under the direction of a civilian at the far end of the square that enlightened them in the end. 'God in heaven,' one of them whispered in awe, 'it's a portable gallows!'

It was.

'A gallows ... a gallows,' the awed whisper went from mouth to mouth. 'They're gonna knot the poor swine up, the lot of them...'

Colonel Katukov, accompanied by the strange civilian with the cold smiling eyes and powerful gloved hands, which he kept rubbing all the time, as if he were washing the dirt from them, explained to the suddenly silent Battalion exactly what he was going to do. 'You filthy Gulag rats think that just because Comrade Stalin,' he said the name as if it were in quotes, 'is in desperate need of men, you can get away with everything and anything. You think you can't be punished

150

because you are too precious; every man is needed in the line. You are wrong. In the line there is no place for traitors and cowards — and trash like that.' He spat into the snow to emphasize his point. 'Now you will see what happens to traitors and cowards in my command.'□

As if they had been waiting just behind the door, four prisoners emerged, clad in long army shirts and nothing else, even their hobbled feet were bare as they shuffled awkwardly through the snow. They halted clumsily next to a ramrod-straight Katukov, trembling either with fear or cold, or perhaps both. The Colonel nodded to the strange civilian.

Slowly, almost pleasurably, the man peeled off his gloves to reveal powerful hands thickly covered with hair, right down to the nails.

Even the Marshal could not quite repress a shudder at the sight of those hands, for now he knew to whom they belonged: a NKVD executioner, the hangman.

The hangman walked slowly to the first prisoner, a slight smile on his face, as if he were pleased to see him, carrying something in his right hand like a dentist holding his pincers concealed in order not to frighten a nervous patient, whose tooth he would soon extract. Suddenly, with startling speed, he darted forward. Before the prisoner could react, the hangman had bound his hands together with the leather strap he had hidden in his hand. From his breast pocket he pulled a white cap and whipped it over the ashen-faced prisoner's head.

'March!' Katukov commanded harshly.

The guard who had appeared now pushed the blindfolded man in the small of the back. He stumbled forward and gently like some kind neighbour helping a blind man across a busy Moscow street, the hangman took his arm and escorted him up the wooden steps of the mobile gallows.

The watching soldiers held their breath. The Marshal shot a glance at Katukov standing there alone in the snow; the colonel wasn't without a heart, he could see that. What was going to happen in a moment affected him too.

Now, while the watchers stared round-eyed in horrified apprehension, the hangman approached the waiting prisoner from behind. Expertly he pulled down the rope noose over the white cap and after squeezing down the rubber washer to hold the noose tight, darted to the wooden lever which would open the trap over which the prisoner now stood.

For an instant the hangman crouched there like a starter about to rush forward, then he called cheerfully, 'dosvedanya' and thrust down the lever.

There was a great gasp from the Gulag rats. One of the prisoners screamed shrilly and fell to his knees in the snow, hands upraised piteously, as the trap clicked open to allow the condemned man to shoot through, the rope twanging taut with the crack of a rifle. Instantly the hangman jumped from the platform and rushed underneath the gallows to where the prisoner was turning round and round in rapid circles. He grabbed the prisoner's legs hanging above his head and pulled hard.

The prisoner's face was hidden by the white bag, but all the same, the onlookers could see from the way the hanging man's chest heaved frantically and the sudden purple flushing of his neck with the veins standing out like writhing worms in it that he was being strangled to death, *slowly*.

Behind the Marshal someone gasped and crossing himself, perhaps the first time he had done so in years, began to say a prayer in a shaky voice that was just short of hysteria.

Then it was over and the other three condemned men were on their knees in the snow, wailing and holding up their hands in supplication, pleading for mercy.

The colonel turned away, as if he could not stand their cowardly faces.

One by one, with the aid of the guards, the smiling hangman led them to the gallows and carried out the execution, speeding each prisoner on his way with a subdued 'good-bye' before rushing down to below to garrotte the unfortunate victim to death.

In the end all four of them swung there in the breeze, their shirts wet and the platform soaked where they had evacuated their bowels with fear and pain, the only sound the stiff creaking of the ropes and the sobbing of one of the Gulag rats in the rear rank. Only then did Colonel Katukov speak again, 'All right, you rabble, you have seen what happens to deserters, you...'

Words failed him. Snapping a contemptuous 'dismiss the pack, Boldin,' over his shoulder, he stamped through the snow to his own quarters, followed by the beaming civilian, who was rubbing his gloved hands again, leaving the bodies swinging in the wind, something hideously incongruous about their skinny white legs protruding from beneath the soaked shirts.

Sick at heart, the Marshal motioned to Teeth. With unaccustomed gentleness for him, Teeth turned, glad to not have to see the hanging men any more, and said, 'All right, you can dismiss now.'

Heads bent, the men trailed away, each and every one of them preoccupied with his own thoughts, leaving the square to the dead. There would be no more desertions in Punishment Battalion 333.

The whores came that very same night. Three truckloads of them. Officially whores had not existed in the Soviet Union since 1920, but as an open-mouthed Teeth exclaimed to an equally amazed Tinleg as the trucks carrying them drew up outside the Battalion Office, 'I know there isn't supposed to be any female meat on the hoof to be bought in Mother Russia these twenty years, my little friend.' He licked his lips in anticipation, as the whores started to descend from the trucks, screeching and giggling, showing ample white thighs, heavy breasts trembling like puddings under their artificial silk blouses. 'But they smell like whores, look like whores —'

'And *are* whores!' Tinleg yelled joyfully, rushing forward towards them, holding the front of his bulging trousers and crying, 'Who's gonna do the pole-vault with me, girls? Who's gonna be first?'

That night the barracks rocked with accordion music, drunken laughter, hysterical screams, as the Gulag rats, drawing water-glasses of vodka straight from the casks of spirits supplied by Zhukov, just as the whores had been, staggered to the piled mattresses at the end of the mess-hall where the score or so of women lay, as drunk as they were themselves, naked save for darned black stockings and their knee-length boots, servicing all who came, performing the same hectic, violent ritual over and over again.

Katukov alone in his quarters save for Vulf, who was as drunk as the rest of the Gulag rats, but who was not interested in the whores, frowned moodily as the screams and laughs penetrated through the blacked-out window. Why did men have to behave like animals before they went into action? he asked himself. Had they no dignity? No belief in the sacredness of their fight, that they had to defile their cause thus?

Vulf, drunk as he was, seemed to be able to read his commander's thoughts, for he said, slurring his words badly, his eyes almost crossed and out of focus, 'It is the tradition, my dear commander. The licentious soldiery are expected to whore before battle. It has been done since time imm … for a long time…'

'Pigs, that's what they are,' Katukov spat out. 'And you, too. Be gone with you and get your dirty snout to the same trough! It will be the last time you do, I warrant.'

Vulf waved his glass at Katukov. 'Ah, but you'll need me, Colonel Katukov one of the … these days. That you will.' He drew a dirty finger across his throat and made a cutting noise. 'For who else will tell you whether they are going to kill you or not, eh…?' With a wicked grin on his drunken face he staggered out, leaving a suddenly sombre Katukov staring at the closed door, wondering just what the spy had meant.

If he had been present at the hushed meeting of his officers some one hundred metres away, each one as sombre and as sober as he was himself, Colonel Katukov would have realized just how serious the threat Vulf had mentioned really was.

'The hangings were the last straw,' Under-Lieutenant Krylov said vehemently, thrusting back the lock of pale blond hair that always fell over his brow when he was excited. 'No other battalion commander would have wasted lives so brutally as that.'

'They were deserters, you know, Krylov,' the Marshal, who headed the secret meeting, reminded the angry young officer softly.

'But would you have hanged them, Boldin?' Piotr, the one-armed commander of the 1st Company, a veteran of the Revolution like himself, who had lost his arm fighting with Budenny's Red Cavalry.

The Marshal shook his head.

'Exactly. Katukov hates us. He takes every and any opportunity to punish us because we are Gulag rats. We could soldier for him from here to Hell and back and still he would not accept us as equals. We are and will always remain traitors and criminals, as far as he is concerned, never soldiers.'

'Ay, you are right there, brother,' a half-dozen officers said angrily, agreeing with the red-faced, one-armed Major.

'Right...' Boldin held his hands up for silence. Gravely he looked from face to face, flushed and angry for the most part. There was a heavy silence inside the room, while from outside came the sound of the drunken carousing of the soldiers and the whores. 'Do I understand you correctly?' he asked after a moment or two.

'You do,' Piotr answered. 'It's either him or us.'

Boldin still wasn't convinced. 'But if he goes, there could well be another commander just as bad.'

'No one can be as bad as that swine. He hasn't got a heart that man.' Piotr hawked and spat angrily on to the dirty floor to emphasize his point.

'You understand what a chance we are taking, brothers?' Boldin persisted.

They nodded. ☐

'A bullet in the back during the first attack and goodbye Colonel Katukov,' someone said. 'It has been done before and the men who did it got away with it.' 'Ay,' Piotr said sagely. 'I lost my first general that way in Galicia in 'fifteen.' He guffawed suddenly, a strange sound in that place where a murder was being arranged. 'The Tsar gave him a hero's funeral back in Petrograd — Leningrad to you bunch of uneducated pigs.'

They laughed politely.

Boldin nodded. 'All right, a show of hands.'

One by one the hands went up. Boldin gazed around the hard determined faces of the men he had fought with and suffered with too in the camps. Slowly he raised his own big scarred paw. 'So be it, then,' he said solemnly.

Outside the shouting continued...

CHAPTER 5

Now it was dawn.

The last of the drunken, staggering whores, some of them almost naked in spite of the sub-zero temperature, had been deposited in the waiting trucks and driven away secretly so that the civilian populace should not become aware that there were such women in their classless, socialist society.

The Marshal, fully dressed, shaven and carrying his equipment, watched half amused as a still drunken Teeth and his little friend Tinleg staggered by, the latter carrying his metal leg over his shoulder from some reason known only to himself. The pair of them would have one hell of a hangover, he told himself, and hoped for their sakes that they had remembered to fill their canteens with the free vodka for the long march ahead of them this day.

He stared at the sky over Moscow. It was grey, sombre and a little threatening, with to the west a faint pink flickering which at some other time he might have thought was lightning. Today he knew better. It was the light of the massed batteries at the front, pounding the Fritzes' positions, in preparation for the great offensive to come.

For some time he stood there in the freezing cold listening to the sounds of the new day, the caw-caw of the rooks, the rattle of the cooks' ladles in the kitchen, the first grumbles of drunken men being roused ungently from a too short sleep, the bark and rasp of men hawking, spitting, clearing their throats, farting. They were the sounds he had lived with most of his life: the sounds of the barracks and men.

Once they had given him pleasure, reminded him that he was one with a great community of fellow men, whom he trusted and who trusted him. But not now. Now they reminded him only of what had been planned the night before, of treachery, base merciless treachery which had robbed him of a career and a family that he had loved dearly, and of the new counter-treachery, that was just as base and merciless. For a moment he thought of Lydia and the hours of happiness with her in the hospital, when he had thought that there might be a chance of making a new start, before he had realized that he carried the Gulag with him wherever he went and always would, like the symptoms of some loathsome disease. There was no hope for him, or anybody else in Punishment Battalion 333 for that matter.

Slowly he became aware that he was not alone on the cold dawn parade ground. He turned.

Katukov was standing at the door of his quarters. Like Boldin, he was fully dressed and carrying his equipment ready to leave and like the other man he, too, was staring at the west. For a moment Boldin wondered what could be going through the big colonel's mind, for his face revealed nothing of his thoughts.

Then Katukov became aware that he was being watched. He turned and his cold gaze lit upon Boldin. He said nothing and the expression on his face did not change, but he knew with the clarity of a vision at that moment what Boldin planned, and Boldin knew he knew. But the big colonel's face showed no fear, nothing save perhaps resignation, as if he might well welcome death in whatever form when it came.

For a long time the two officers stared at each other wordlessly across the parade ground until the trumpet sounding reveille finally broke their reverie and Katukov, the victim, called to the man who would murder him as soon as he had the opportunity, 'Comrade Major, have the men ready to march within the hour!'

The band, ten abreast, marched proudly across Red Square, filling it with the glare and silver blare of their instruments. Behind them followed the battalions, the regiments, the brigades, the divisions, the corps, thousands upon thousands of marching men, heading for the west and the front. The stamp of their steel-shod boots echoed and re-echoed back and forth across the square.

No one watched them, save the NKVD men, standing shoulder to shoulder to guard the man above them on the balcony. No one cheered. No one waved a flag. They were going to their deaths unhonoured and unsung, save for the final salute of that lone man standing high above them out of bullet-range, his arm raised limply each time a new formation stamped back.

Now Colonel Katukov came almost parallel with the little man on the balcony. He raised his curved sabre and bellowed hoarsely, 'Punishment Battalion 333 — PARADE MARCH... EYES RIGHT...'

Woodenly the thousand men from the Gulag raised their legs almost to waist-height, swinging their left arms across their chests to the rifles held tightly in their right hands, heads clicking, as if on springs, to the right.

Boldin swept his sword round across his chest and stared upwards. For a moment he caught a glimpse of that yellow, pock-marked inscrutable face and felt a great hate course through his body. Stalin! The man who had nearly destroyed Russia. For that man he was now marching to the front to fight and perhaps die. Then Katukov was crying, 'EYES FRONT...' and Stalin was gone.

They were on their way. Punishment Battalion 333 was marching to battle once more...

BOOK FIVE: *HEIGHT 444*

'And remember — keep a tight arsehole, boys!'
Colonel Hardt to the Stalin Scholars

CHAPTER 1

A thin mist writhed eerily over the surface of the Volga Dam, lurking around the snow-covered bushes at its bank, curling through the firs which bordered the path. In single file and placing down their feet with care so that the sound of their boots crunching on the hard snow would not alert the Fritzes dug in on the far bank somewhere, they followed the bright young lieutenant of Intelligence who was to be their guide for the trip down the canal. The silver night was silent save for the steady croak of the frogs in the middle of the ice-free water and the mysterious splashes of some night creature or other. Yet the very silence was frightening and Boldin up at point with Katukov was tempted more than once to look behind to check whether they were being followed.

'Here we stop,' the lieutenant whispered, as if the nearest Fritz were ten metres away instead of a hundred. 'Pass it on please, Comrade Colonel.'

Dutifully Katukov passed on the order and it went slowly down the long column until finally they were all crouched in the grey-fogged undergrowth, hearts beating excitedly, weapons held at the ready, eyes keen and searching.

A flare rose gracefully on the other side of the dam and hung there above the mist like a silver star.

'Freeze!' the lieutenant ordered.

They froze.

But the flare sank without the expected cry of alarm, followed by a burst of machine-gun fire. They had not been spotted — yet.

The lieutenant licked dry lips and briefed them once again. 'The Fascists are dug in over there.' He pointed across the dam, but they could make out nothing because of the grey mist. 'Take my word for it, anyway. Now if we can successfully launch the boats without alarming them, I think we can be on our own way and in position by dawn so that we can lie up for the rest of the day. There is only one problem.' He fell silent, as yet another German flare rushed into the night sky, indicating just how nervous the enemy was.

Only one problem, the Marshal told himself. That was the understatement of 1941! Zhukov expected them to take a whole battalion from the Volga Dam, along twenty kilometres of canal, one bank of which was held by the Fritzes, land without being spotted on their side of the canal, dig in for the day right in the middle of the enemy and begin their attack on his massed tanks the following night. He smiled wanly at the tense young Intelligence officer as the flare started to fade. There wasn't just one problem — there were a score of them!

The lieutenant continued. 'Now, with this mist I am pretty confident that we will be able to launch the boats without the Fascist sentries over there spotting us, but there *is* the problem of not being detected where the Volga Canal links up with the dam.'

'What do you mean, Lieutenant?' Katukov asked suspiciously, almost as if the young officer might attempt to sabotage this operation which he had promised Marshal Zhukov personally the day before would be successful.

'Well, Comrade Colonel, the dam narrows there, so even if we keep to this bank as close as we can, the German sentries will be, at the most, only twenty metres away.'

Katukov absorbed the information with a frown. That was close indeed. He hadn't realized that the waterway narrowed to that extent. But when he spoke, the colonel's voice revealed none of his doubts and fears. 'The men will be quiet. Anyone who makes a noise and gives our position away to the Fascists will be disciplined most severely — *shot* in other words.'

The young lieutenant smiled warily. 'With all due respect, Comrade Colonel, if that eventuality arises, I think it will be the Fritzes who will be doing the disciplining. At that range even a one-eyed Fascist pig couldn't miss.'

'Oh, come on,' Katukov said impatiently, 'let's not stop gossiping here like peasant women at a village market. Where are the boats now?'

Five minutes later the first Gulag rats started to crawl into the little rubber and canvas assault boats which Soviet Intelligence had concealed in the reeds at their side of the dam the night before. Time passed leadenly, while Boldin and a little group including Teeth and Tinleg, manning the Battalion's heavy machine-guns, stared tensely across the bank of low mist at the other side, waiting for the first cry of alarm which would spell disaster.

None came. Instead the Intelligence lieutenant, his boots dripping wet, came back to where they were positioned and reported, 'All ready to move off, Comrade Major. It's your turn now. I'll take you down.' Boldin frowned. 'Are you coming with us?'

'Yes. I was brought up not a *verst* from here in a small village before I went to the university. I know the canal like the back of my hand. Besides I've been on the staff since the autumn.' He grinned up at the Marshal. 'I'll get a medal for this one — it'll impress my girl.'

The Marshal returned the young man's frank smile, though the latter's presence was unwelcome. When the time of reckoning with Katukov came, he wanted no witnesses from outside the Battalion. The Intelligence lieutenant meant postponing Colonel Katukov's "death-in-action" for another day. 'All right, you hero, lead on,' he said.

Five minutes later the little flotilla was under way.

Cautiously, very cautiously, hardly daring to breathe, they paddled down the centre of the dam, any sound they made muffled by the wet dripping mist which clung to the surface of the water. All the same every one of them knew that if the unseen watchers on the other bank spotted them now they would be sitting ducks, virtually powerless to defend themselves, a machine-gunner's dream target. It would be a massacre.

Bringing up the rear in the final boat, Boldin, squatting awkwardly next to the Intelligence lieutenant, peered through the gloom trying to see what lay ahead. But all he could see was the shadowy outline of the little boat ahead.

The lieutenant grinned at him.

'*Sobatchnia dusha!*' the Marshal hissed, 'what are you looking so happy about?'

'I was thinking of the look on the Fritzes' fat faces when we turn up in their midst, Comrade Major.'

'We've got to get there first, Comrade Lieutenant,' Boldin said sourly and continued his anxious vigil.

Now the current, which had hardly existed up to then, started to pick up as they approached the spot where the Volga Canal exited from the dam and the width of the water began to narrow. Like most Russians, the Marshal was no sailor and as the little boat commenced rocking, he fought desperately to hold down the sour bile in his throat. In front of him, Teeth, his gleaming steel dental plates held carefully in his big right hand, was being sick over the side, watched by an amused young lieutenant.

The speed of their boats increased even more as the narrow entrance to the canal started to loom up out of the grey gloom. Trying to keep noise down to a minimum and at the same time to avoid disaster, as the boats were swept by the foaming white water towards one or other of the two banks, the now sweating Gulag rats fought with their paddles to keep themselves in the middle of the waterway. Boldin, feeling helpless, watched as the entrance to the Volga Canal came ever closer. Now they could not be more than ten or fifteen metres from the German side of the water. He narrowed his eyes to slits and tried to penetrate the grey gloom which lay there. But he couldn't. For all he could make out, there could be a hundred Fritzes over there, squatting behind their machine-guns, waiting happily for them to come level with their sights. He swallowed hard and dismissed that frightening thought quickly. Whether they were there or not, there was nothing he could do about it now.

'Stop paddling,' a soft voice called from the boat ahead. 'Let the current carry you.'

Obediently the men in Boldin's boat carried out the order, crouching low in a pathetic effort to present the lowest possible silhouette — just in case. Now the flotilla swept towards the entrance unguided, swept round and about by the current, every man's heart racing like a trip hammer, body tense for the sudden impact of red-hot lead which *must* strike the soft flesh at any moment now.

Boldin swallowed hard and raised his head cautiously over the gunwale. He could see the bank on the German side quite clearly now in a hole in the layer of mist: the usual dirty steep rise of frozen mud and ice-rimmed bullrushes. But there was no sign of the enemy. Perhaps they weren't manning the whole length of the waterway? Perhaps they didn't have enough troops and were relying on their usual "hedgehog" method of defending large stretches of terrain? Perhaps —

His heart missed a beat as their little boat lurched into some unseen underwater object with a noise that surely must wake up the dead and came to a halt. Before them the other boat disappeared into the mist.

'Son-of-a-whore,' the lieutenant cursed, the fear apparent in his voice, 'what's up?'

'We're stuck — that's what's up!' Teeth mumbled through toothless gums.

'Paddles —'

'For God's sake, no paddles!' Boldin cut in harshly. 'They'll hear us!'

'Well, what are we going to do, Major?' the lieutenant hissed urgently as the water rushed by them on both sides, but not able to free the boat from whatever was holding them there, stranded just under the enemy's nose.

'This.' Taking a deep breath, Boldin freed himself of his pistol, and went over the side. The icy water took his breath away and he nearly cried out with the freezing numbing pain of it. But he caught himself just in time and fighting the current, hands holding on to the boat fervently, he sought for hold on the slippery pebbles below. He found it in the same instant that Teeth braved the water to do the same, whispering, 'Major, I think this is gonna freeze the hell out of my plumbing.'

Boldin nodded his agreement and concentrated on getting a good hold, as the water rushed and tumbled, spuming up whitely around his waist. 'Push!' he commanded through gritted teeth. They pushed. Nothing happened. The little boat remained firmly where it was.

They took the strain again and pushed with all their strength, the veins standing out at the temples an ugly purple with the effort. Again the boat refused stubbornly to move.

'Try a —' Boldin broke off. A light had penetrated the grey gloom of the opposite bank.

'Shit!' Teeth whispered urgently. '*Fritzes!*'

'Duck everybody ... perfectly still now,' Boldin commanded in a voice he hardly recognized as his own, as the light started to sweep their way slowly, casually, as if the man holding the torch was not yet alerted to their presence, was carrying out some sort of routine search.

Hardly daring to breathe, his face almost level with the fast-flowing water, holding on to the boat with grim determination, Boldin and Teeth waited for what must happen. The beam got ever closer. Boldin tensed. The water just in front of his nose was bright with light. *This was it!*

Nothing happened. For what seemed an age they were trapped by the light, held there like a moth attracted to a bright flame, and then it was gone and they were left panting, as if they had just run a great race.

In a cracked voice, Teeth said, 'I've just pissed in my right boot.'

'I wasn't far off either,' Boldin agreed and raising his head, stared at the opposite bank. But the man with the torch had gone and the mist was beginning to curl upwards and cover the bank once more. Luck was on their side. For some reason they had not been spotted.

Boldin knew they wouldn't be lucky the second time; the man with the torch must have been blind not to have seen them. 'Come on, Teeth,' he urged, 'now really put your back into it and let's get off this damned rock.'

'Ready when you are, Comrade Major.'

'Ready now.' Boldin heaved, grunting in the fashion of teamsters urging their straining horses to drag a heavy log out of the forest, 'hey-*rup* ... hey-*rup*!'

At his side, Teeth strained too, his massive muscles bulging through his soaked uniform, as he applied all his great strength in one last desperate attempt to free the boat before they were spotted for good. The boat started to budge.

'*More* ... *more*...' Boldin said urgently. 'Come on, all you've got!'

They heaved and then in one great rush, the boat was moving off freely once more, gathering speed at every instant as the current caught it, and they were being hauled and half-dragged, soaked, frozen and exhausted over the gunwale in the very same moment as the little craft cleared the dam and swept down into the Volga Canal. They had successfully cleared obstacle number one.

CHAPTER 2

Katukov stumbled through the waist-deep water, accompanied by the young Intelligence officer. The mist still covered them, though a worried anxious Katukov thought his men were making a devil of a row as they waded towards the enemy-held bank. Behind him one of the Gulag rats carrying a heavy machine-gun on his shoulder disappeared into a pothole and came up spluttering and gasping for air noisily.

'In the devil's name,' he hissed, 'don't make so much damned noise, will you!'

'Perhaps the Fritzes will be in the hay,' the lieutenant attempted to pacify him, as the two men started to climb up the slippery steep bank.

'Perhaps,' Katukov grunted, unloosening his holster flap as they reached the top, and paused while Piotr in charge of Number One Company brought up his men and lined the bank.

'All present and correct,' he reported *sotto voce* a few moments later. Again Katukov grunted, his gaze concentrated on what little he could see ahead of him.

Piotr turned and returned to his men to wait for further orders, nodding significantly to a soaked Boldin as he appeared over the bank and made his way to report to Katukov.

Boldin knew what that nod meant. Katukov was alone save for the young Intelligence officer up front. It would be as easy as falling off a log to deal with him now. Boldin pulled a face. The time was opportune, but getting rid of Katukov now would mean "liquidating", as the NKVD put it, the young officer too. That would be the only way to seal his lips safely.

But if the coldblooded murder of Katukov went against the grain, that of the young Intelligence officer was even more repugnant to Boldin. No, he decided as he walked forward, dripping water, Katukov would live another day.

Katukov took in his wet uniform, but said nothing about it. Instead, he ordered: 'Take those two rogues of NCOs with you, Boldin. Recce the ground. Their first position can't be far from here, though in this damn fog, it could be a million kilometres away for all we would know, and eradicate it. There must be no sound. Then I'll bring up the rest of the Battalion. Clear, Boldin?'

'Clear,' Boldin echoed dutifully, as if he were some greenhorn of a under-lieutenant who had never been in action before instead of a full Marshal of the Soviet Union and a veteran of half a dozen bloody campaigns. Without another word, he turned and placed his hand on his helmet, fingers outspread, the infantry signal for 'rally on me'. Teeth and Tinleg hurriedly joined him.

Swiftly he outlined their mission, while Katukov looked on impatiently, knowing that time was running out rapidly. Soon it would be dawn and if the sun appeared, it would soon burn away the fog.

'Good luck,' the lieutenant wished them as they disappeared into the fog.

Katukov merely grunted.

A moment later they had gone and all was tense silence again on the bank of the Volga Canal.

The sentry yawned and wondered when he was going to be relieved. It had been a damned long two hours "on" and he was cold and parched. Even a cup of German Army ersatz coffee would be very welcome at this moment. It would warm him up at least.

Suddenly he started.

A slow figure was coming towards him out of the gloom, hobbling along with difficulty, as if he were some kind of cripple. The sentry brought up his bayoneted rifle, instantly awake. The man approaching him was definitely a Russian.

'*Wer da?*' he challenged harshly, wondering what the devil the little Russki cripple was doing wandering through the forest at that time of the morning.

The stranger halted instantly. '*Ne ponimayu pa nmetski!*' he quavered in Russian, head bent humbly, supporting himself with the aid of a rough stick, obviously cut from a tree.

'*Davoi*, advance and be recognized!' the sentry commanded gruffly, with a jerk of his rifle, recovering from his surprise and telling himself that the little Russki was probably one of the many who had been wounded in the summer and was supporting himself by begging and stealing, as was the custom with ex-Red Army men too crippled to do any more fighting for Uncle Joe.

Shoulders bent humbly, the cripple advanced, eyes on the ground as if afraid to look at the conqueror.

The sentry spat contemptuously. They were all like this, the Popovs. One good German fart and they all ran with their tails between their legs. Idly he wondered why the shitting High Command was taking so long to beat 'em; he and a couple of his cronies could have done it with one arm tied behind their backs.

'*Halt!*' he barked.

The Popov halted. He had understood the tone, even if he had not understood the German word. He stood there patiently, waiting till the sentry deigned to speak to him.

The German took his time, sucking in his fat belly, every inch the Aryan superman, as Goebbels invariably described the German soldier in Russia, confronted by the third-class sub-human; didn't their very name seem to suggest "slave"? Slav — slave, it was all the same.

'Got any booze?' he barked.

The Russian cripple didn't answer.

'Vodka,' he said. '*Gdrya vodka?*'

The cripple raised his head, a light of understanding in his dark eyes.

The sentry beamed. All the Popovs carried vodka with them; they couldn't live without their booze. He licked his cracked lips in anticipation, as the cripple reached into his shabby uniform blouse to fetch out the bottle.

But it was not a bottle that Tinleg pulled out. Instead a screw of newspaper appeared in his dirty paw.

'Hey, what's this —'

The sentry's question ended in a scream as the black pepper exploded in his eyes, blinding him. The very next instant the little man's stout "crutch" smashed across his chest. The German gave a great gasp and bent double. It was the opportunity that Tinleg had been waiting for. His "crutch" crashed down on the back of the German's neck, just below the rim of the coal-scuttle helmet. The sentry hit the ground as if pole-axed. He didn't make another sound.

Tinleg caught his breath for a moment, his anxious gaze surveying the forest all around for other Fritzes. There were none in the immediate vicinity, but they were there somewhere. Of that he was sure. But for the moment they were safe. He thrust his two fingers into his mouth and whistled shrilly.

The Marshal and Teeth, weapons in their hands, appeared almost immediately. Teeth looked down at the unconscious or dead German and said, 'I thought you'd never croak the bastard.'

Tinleg made an obscene gesture, with his middle finger. 'Sit on that, you fat-arsed bastard.'

The Marshal grinned. 'You did very well, Tinleg. That pepper trick worked well.' His grin vanished. 'All right now, let's find their camp and get on with the business. It'll be dawn soon and we don't want their relief coming and finding his comrade having a little sleep like this, do we?'

They moved into the trees like grey predatory timber wolves.

The Marshal sniffed the air, trying to determine the nature of the strange pungent odour, while his two companions crouching in the frozen bushes stared at the tented camp in front of them.

There were about six of them, camouflaged well as was always the case with the Fritzes, and in the gloom the watchers could make out the tyre tracks of many vehicles in the rutted frozen snow. But there was no sign of the tanks they had half expected to find there. Indeed it seemed a very unmilitary establishment altogether, for there were no other sentries visible. The only sentry to guard the whole camp was the one that Tinleg had dealt with.

'Be a good place for the Battalion to hide up for the day in, Comrade Major,' Teeth whispered thoughtfully. 'Isolated and all that and it doesn't look like any kind of main camp. There'd be more activity than this at this time of the morning. There's only one tent where the Fritzes seem to be awake.' He indicated the central tent from which came the faint yellow glow through the canvas of a shaded lantern.

The Marshal nodded his agreement, still sniffing the air, trying to ascertain what the smell could be.

Then he had it. It was ether! 'You know what this place is, brothers?' he asked, a plan already beginning to form in his mind.

They shook their heads.

'A frontline field dressing station.'

'Of course,' Tinleg agreed. 'Otherwise the Fritzes wouldn't have tents this far forward.'

'Yes,' the Marshal said. 'They've obviously built the camp here, right up front, ready for their next offensive. Obviously they're not scared we'll overrun it.' He smiled suddenly. 'Well, I think our Fritz sawbones are in for a little surprise, eh, brothers?' They returned his smile.

The Marshal was business-like again. 'All right, Teeth, off you go and bring up the Battalion. Tinleg and I will keep this place under observation.'

Teeth looked troubled. 'You'll be all right, Comrade Major?' □

'Of course,' the Marshal answered easily. 'Who could cause trouble for a couple of hairy-arsed old vets like this one-legged rogue and me? Not a bunch of fat-bellied German bone-menders, that's for certain! Now be off with you.'

Tinleg looked up at a worried Teeth and grinned wolfishly with his mouthful of long yellow fangs. 'Now run along like a good boy and don't talk to any stranger offering you sweets, will you now, sonny?'

Teeth muttered something about Tinleg performing an unnatural act with his mother and went reluctantly. At the edge of the forest he looked back. The two of them crouched there looking confident enough. He nodded his head. Everything would be all right, he told himself.

But for once Teeth was wrong. One hour later he was back with the rest of the Battalion.

But the Marshal and Tinleg had vanished and the camp was deserted…

CHAPTER 3

'Deserters, do you think, *Herr Stabsarzt*?' General von Manteuffel asked, looking at the two sullen prisoners, the one who was a cripple nursing a nasty swelling at the back of his head where the sentry had smashed the metal butt of his rifle down upon it.

'No, definitely not, *Herr General*,' the self-important, fat-bellied doctor with the gold-rimmed pince-nez answered. 'They were both armed when we captured them.' He beamed at the little general.

Von Manteuffel smiled. The sawbones was obviously very pleased with his capture; one might have thought he had put a whole Ivan division in the bag. He turned to the interpreter, a Volga-German, who had deserted to the division at the beginning of the invasion of Russia. 'Ask them what they were doing in the woods, Sergei.'

The blond young Russian rapped out the general's question. 'Now hurry up!' he snapped, when they didn't answer.

The Marshal looked at him coldly, while Tinleg raised himself slightly from his stool and gave a long, contemptuous fart.

Sergei flushed and started to explain. Manteuffel held up his hand, slightly amused by the cripple's reaction. 'You don't have to tell me, Sergei. They're obviously not talking.'

'*Jawohl, Herr General*. But with the general's permission, I think I could — er — persuade them to co-operate soon enough.' He bent down and drew his knife deliberately from the side of his right boot, his dark eyes fixed threateningly.

'No, no, Sergei,' Manteuffel said hastily. 'I will not tolerate that kind of nasty business in my division.' He looked around the faces of his staff officers and saw confirmation of his attitude there, although they, like himself, would have dearly loved to know what the Russians had been doing skulking around the field dressing station. 'I think we shall leave those methods to the gentlemen in brown, eh?'

There was a low murmur of agreement from his officers.

Manteuffel looked at the bigger of the two prisoners, from his insignia obviously a major. The man was older than the average *Wehrmacht* major, and the sabre scars on his brawny arms could only have been incurred in a much older war than this. The man's face, hard and set, seemed oddly familiar too. Where had he seen it before?

Manteuffel played a sudden hunch. Looking directly at the prisoner, he said in German, 'You will be well treated as befits an officer prisoner if you will tell me this — why were you in the forest this morning?'

The Marshal hesitated, yet the temptation was too great for him to overcome. 'Herr von Manteuffel,' he said in slow, careful German, 'I think if you were in my place now, you would refuse to answer that question.' There was a gasp of amazement from the watching officers. Manteuffel stared too. 'You know me?' he managed to stutter.

'Yes. You were one of the German officers who trained with us in the days of the Black Reichswehr back in 1930, not a million kilometres from here either.'

Now von Manteuffel remembered. The bold Soviet Tank Corps general who supervised the illegal training of the old pre-Hitler Army in the days when the Western Allies had spies everywhere in Germany. 'General ... no.' — What was the rank later? — '*Marshal Vladimir Boldin?*'

The prisoner nodded his head quietly.

Almost immediately excited chatter filled the peasant hut which served as von Manteuffel's divisional headquarters. 'A real Ivan marshal,' the staff officers exclaimed. 'Boldin, one of the heroes of the Revolution... What in three devils' name is he doing wandering around the forest behind our lines like this...?'

Manteuffel held up his hands for peace. '*Meine Herren, bitte* ... please gentlemen...'

The chatter died away and von Manteuffel stared at his prisoner, taking in the dirty uniform devoid of any decorations and Boldin's taut, emaciated face, that of a man who had suffered a great deal. 'You were purged with the rest in the late thirties, weren't you? I remembered reading about it in our papers ... I felt sorry for you.'

'Thank you,' the Marshal said softly.

'And now you are fighting as an infantry officer. What happened, Marshal?'

'It's a long story, Herr von Manteuffel,' Boldin answered, realizing suddenly that his impulse was paying dividends. Now the German was intrigued by his abrupt transformation from Marshal of the Red Army to ordinary infantry major. For the moment he had forgotten the question of what they were doing lurking around behind the German front.

'We have some time, Marshal,' von Manteuffel said politely. 'It does not appear that — er — the Red Army is ready to attack us at this particular moment.'

There was mild laughter from his officers; they knew the Red Army was virtually finished. Soon their own tanks would be moving again and then nothing could stop them capturing Moscow.

Boldin thought of the Gulag rats hiding in the forest not more than a kilometre away from this very HQ and knew he must somehow keep the Fritzes guessing until Katukov had a chance to carry out his mission. 'I am not as young as I used to be, Herr General,' he sighed. 'Perhaps if I were allowed some food and a drink — and the same for my batman,' — he indicated Tinleg, who was staring from one face to the other, completely mystified by the course events had taken — 'then I might be prepared better to tell you my — er — sad story.'

'Why, of course, Marshal,' von Manteuffel said hastily, repressing his curiosity quickly. 'Naturally you shall be given food. Then we can talk.' He clapped his hands loudly.

His orderly appeared at the door.

'*Ordonanz, zu essen und zu trinken für den russischen Herren. Sofort!*' he rasped in that nasal Prussian accent of his.

'*Sofort, Herr General!*' The soldier clicked his heels together smartly and disappeared.

Boldin breathed out a sigh of relief. For the time being the Battalion was saved. Von Manteuffel, gentleman that he was, would not expect him to answer questions while he was eating. Now it was up to Katukov and the Gulag rats.

Piotr rubbed his big hand across his unshaven, bristling chin. 'What now, Comrade Colonel?' he asked a thoughtful Katukov.

Teeth strained anxiously for the colonel's answer.

Katukov stared at the hastily deserted camp. It did not take a clairvoyant to realize that Boldin and the NCO had been captured. The question now was what the Fritzes would do with their two captives.

He knew that they did not even bother to interrogate the rank-and-file of their Red Army captives. □

But Boldin was a major and surely they would be curious about his presence behind their lines.

'I don't think Major Boldin will talk easily,' Piotr said slowly, expressing Katukov's own unspoken thoughts. 'He is a brave one, the Marshal. But the Fritzes have a certain reputation.' He glanced keenly at a silent Katukov. 'They are said to be able to make a mummy talk in the end.' He could not resist the sneer, his hatred of Katukov was so great. 'And you, Comrade Colonel, know with your experience that every man, however brave and loyal he may be, has his breaking-point in the end?'

Katukov flushed. He knew the damned impertinent company commander was referring to his own organization, the NKVD. Didn't the swine know that torture was only used in the last resort and at the explicit order of no less a person than Beria himself? Besides, he, personally, had never allowed himself to be involved in that kind of piggery. But there was no time for explanations and recriminations now. The company commander was right. In the end Boldin would talk. Besides, what else could one expect from a Gulag rat? Now every minute was important if they were going to carry out their mission.

'Listen, Major,' he rapped, 'we'll split the Battalion into companies. Each company will take one of the designated areas and deal with the tanks laagered there.'

Piotr looked at him in sudden alarm. 'In broad daylight, Comrade Colonel? But —'

'In broad daylight,' Katukov cut him short brutally. 'There'll be no hiding out till darkness now. They'd find us long before then. Dangerous as it is, we'll just have to take that risk. Understood?'

'Understood,' Piotr answered woodenly. 'And then, Comrade Colonel, back across the canal?'

'No,' Katukov answered firmly. 'That is what they would expect us to do.' He swung round on the young officer from Intelligence. 'Lieutenant, you are the expert on the area, what is the best defensive feature within a radius of a kilometre or so?'

The young officer thought for a moment, then he remembered the hill where he had had his first experience of sex with a plump, big-bosomed peasant girl from the local *kolhoz*, who had nearly choked the life out of him with her strong-armed passion. Carried away with ecstasy, he with his pants down to his ankles and she with her skirt thrown up about her face, they had rolled right down the steep hillside that fine summer's day so long ago, to collapse, all passion spent, at the bottom. 'Passion point,' he said.

'What did you say?'

The lieutenant flushed to the roots of his hair. 'Sorry, Comrade Colonel, that's a local name. It just slipped out. Height 444.'

Both Katukov and Piotr lifted their leather-bound map cases and stared at the map of the local area until they had located the hill feature. Katukov pursed his lips as he studied the contours. 'Not bad,' he said finally, 'not bad, Lieutenant.'

'Steep slopes on all three sides, with the fourth running down to the canal,' Piotr agreed. 'An excellent defensive position.'

'And it's only wooded on the one side, Comrade Colonel,' the lieutenant said. 'At least it was when I was last there — er — some time ago now.' He thought abruptly of those big breasts which had threatened to swamp him when she had undone her bodice and swallowed hard. 'Good fields of — er — fire.'

Katukov made his decision. 'Then Height 444 it is.' He flashed a glance at his army wristwatch. 'We break up immediately, carry out our tasks and assemble there at zero twelve hundred hours. The offensive across the canal is scheduled to start this very night. We must hold out till then.'

'Many will be killed, Colonel,' Piotr said, forgetting his hatred of Katukov and thinking of his men who would have to bear the inevitable losses. □

There are plenty more Gulag rats in the camps, Major,' Katukov said coldly. 'Now get on with it. Time is running out. You, Lieutenant, will come with me. Sergeant-major,' he called, not waiting for the Intelligence officer to react, 'get me —' He stopped short.

Teeth, who had been standing there listening only a moment before, had vanished.

CHAPTER 4

The Gulag rats caught the men of the 7th Panzer Division by complete surprise. That morning they ranged far and wide behind the German lines, destroying tank laager after laager, setting petrol dumps alight, wrecking communications, exploding the forest trails which the enemy would use to bring up his armour in any advance.

One hour after they had started their raid, two of Manteuffel's tank battalions had lost most of their tanks, all of their petrol and oil dumps and a major ammunition store, which Major Piotr's explosives experts detonated with a great rending crash that seemed to go on for ever.

'Easy as falling off a log,' the delighted Gulag rats cried to one another as they ran down yet another column of burning German tanks, heaving Molotov cocktails to left and right, careless of the enemy slugs winging their way. 'What does Old Leather-Face need those soldier-boys of his for when he's got the Punishment Battalion?'

By ten, panic had set in among Manteuffel's formations. Grossly distorted, panic-stricken reports were flooding into his headquarters from all sides. *'The Russians are attacking in divisional strength... Soviet dive-bombers hitting us with multiple incendiaries... Ivan para troops dropping right on top of our positions...'*

'Heaven, arse and cloudburst!' a crimson-faced, worried Manteuffel exploded, as yet another alarmist report was handed to him by an ashen staff officer, 'you might think the whole damn Red Army was attacking us!'

One hour later the Gulag rats were still on the rampage. But now they were after other things than tanks and petrol dumps.

In the 1st Company they had discovered a German supply dump. The fat bespectacled German quartermaster had tried to defend it single-handed and they had riddled him with M.G. fire so that he now lay spread-eagled over a pile of salami sausages, soaking them with his blood, as if he had died fighting to save that symbol of German *Kultur*, the sausage, while the whooping, triumphant, half-starved Gulag rats looted his precious stores, ransacking the shelves, ripping open the cupboards, shooting off the padlocks of the drawers, crying out in rapture at every new delicacy they discovered.

It was then that they discovered the *schnapps*, great fifty-litre carboys of it, protected by wickerwork cages, so heavy that they needed all their strength to lift them to their lips. But lift them they did, taking huge draughts of the fiery pale liquid coughing and spluttering, the *schnapps* running down their unshaven chins, tugging the carboys from each other, fighting to get at the *schnapps*.

It was about this time that men of the 1st Company, as drunk as their comrades of the 2nd who had first discovered the German supply dump, came across the "grey mice".

A huge German woman tried to bar their way to the *Wehrmacht's* nurses' quarters in the tented camp. Her arms outstretched across her massive field-grey bosom, she tried to halt their drunken progress in vain. They burst into the screaming women's quarters. The Gulag rats brooked no opposition. They slapped the "grey mice" into submission, forcing them down on the floor, ears deaf to their screams for mercy. This day there was to be no mercy for the Fritzes.

But by now Manteuffel's reserve battalion had been alerted and was beginning to counter-attack with the Germans' usual speed in such matters. Alarmed and well aware that once panic broke out, his men could well be swept into the canal itself, Katukov reacted hastily. Together with the Intelligence lieutenant and a small HQ section of riflemen, he held off the Germans' first thrust and ordered the rest of his spread-out companies to begin withdrawing to Height 444, each company to take its turn in the rear guard, while its neighbour slipped through it, fighting and retreating, giving ground only very slowly.

But the hard-pressed colonel, manning one of the HQ section's heavy machine-guns with the lieutenant, was unaware of the state of discipline in his companies, with most of the men blind drunk by now.

Major Piotr of the 1st Company was aware. He burst into the "grey mice" camp to find four of his men, naked save for their boots and helmets, rifles thrown carelessly to one side, attacking a screaming German nurse. Beside himself with rage he lashed about him with his knout, stripping the flesh from their naked white backs in great bloody streaks. Yet even the pain did not seem able to stop them and the others; they were too drunk to notice.

He fired his pistol into the air. The wild orgy continued. 'Stop this!' he bellowed, crimson-faced. '*Yo tuoyu mat!*' he cursed, '*stop it!*'

The only response was from a drunken private squatting in his own vomit in the corner, guzzling schnapps from his helmet, who raised it as if in toast, his eyes unable to focus, and slurred '*nastroyva pan!*'

Piotr knew that only the most drastic of actions would stop the drunken orgy. Already he could hear the snap-and-crackle of small-arms fire getting ever closer and he didn't need to be clairvoyant to realize that the Fritzes were counter-attacking. He hesitated no longer. 'All right, you swine, now stop it! I'll count to three and then I'm going to fire!'

His words made no impression whatsoever in that screaming chaos. '*One ... two ... three...*'

Piotr seized the machine pistol from the nerveless fingers of his wide-eyed orderly and pressed the trigger. The weapon leaped into frenetic life. Slugs hissed from it. Men went down everywhere, bloody holes stitched along their white backs, dying and choking in their own blood, spines arching in one last frenzied paroxysm.

Shaking almost uncontrollably, Piotr flung the machine pistol back at the orderly and strode into the centre of the suddenly awed, silent, and now completely sober, mess of bodies, kicking the survivors to their feet, ignoring the sobbing, hysterical grey mice, who lay there. 'Come on, you pigs!' he cried. 'The Fascists are coming... Move it now... *Move it...*'

Teeth was glad of the confusion everywhere, as he worked his way carefully and stealthily into the German farmhouse HQ, ducking swiftly every time heavy boots ran by or the green and white signal flares, which the Fritzes were shooting off to summon aid, hissed into the morning sky. Everywhere there was alarm and confusion. Bugles blew. Officers' whistles shrilled. NCOs barked orders, engines burst into noisy life. Riders spread on to the motorbikes and started them with a roar. But the din could not hide the crescendo of the ever-increasing fire fight to his rear. The Battalion had run into trouble and if they were going to find the Marshal and Tinleg and free them, he knew that they would have to do it soon, damned soon!

He moved on, scenting potential danger everywhere, but always avoiding it, realizing as he did so that his own stained uniform did not look very different from that of the field-greys in this light. He passed a detail of Red Army prisoners stolidly digging a mass grave for German dead, apparently unmoved by the fact that their comrades-in-arms were so near. He ducked and crawled along the neat line of German corpses, bodies rigid and motionless, eyes staring unseeingly at the grey winter sky. Even in death, he told himself, the Fritzes were on parade. Straightening up, now that he was out of sight of the sentry guarding the Russian POWs, he took stock of his surroundings.

The farmhouse in which the HQ was located was to his right. Around it, well camouflaged with typical Fritz thoroughness, there were the tents which housed the staff and essential services. He sniffed, knowing that he would have to make a move soon. Remain standing here long and he would be discovered by some nosey Fritz or other. *Where would they keep their prisoners?*

Then he had it. Not in the farmhouse or the tents of course. There in the loft above the pigsty, which was now hidden from curious eyes by a screen of hessian sacking, for the prudish Germans were obviously using it for a latrine. Why else the sentry? They didn't put sentries even in front of officers' crappers! It *had* to be the place! Teeth made his decision. Hiding his Red Army forage cap, adorned with an enamel red star, inside his blouse, he ripped open his belt and started forward hurriedly, fumbling with the flies of his breeches as if he were in desperate need.

'*Den flatten Otto, Kamerad?*' the sentry asked, grinning at the big man's plight, in spite of the alarming volume of fire from nearby.

Teeth mumbled something and staggered inside behind the screen of hessian.

A long, many-holed board stretched in front of him, supported at intervals by empty ration-boxes. He wrinkled his nose at the stink of human faeces and lime and told himself it was the familiar eighteen-hole crapper common also to the Red Army. 'Even the Fritzes shit the same as we do,' he commented and then turned his attention to the ceiling of the old pigsty above him.

It was of the usual wattle-and-mud construction used by the farmers of the Volga region and he told himself it shouldn't be too difficult to break through. Without any further hesitation he sprang on to the seat of the nearest crapper and, slipping out his bayonet, attacked the ceiling.

Within minutes he had already cleared a respectable hole in the ceiling, his shoulders and the seat of the crapper below covered in ancient plaster and bits of broken blackened wood. His forehead covered in a film of greasy sweat now from his efforts, Teeth hacked away at the hole, enlarging it speedily, praying that the sentry outside was the only one guarding the prisoners, who had to be somewhere above him. *They had to be*, for he knew he would not get a second chance. Outside the fire-fight had passed its crescendo and was now beginning to die away, as Major Piotr and the other company commanders who were still alive rallied their drunken subordinates and began the withdrawal to the Height.

And then finally the hole in the ceiling was big enough for the huge NCO to put his head through. Grasping hold of the nearest rafter, he pulled himself up and poked his head through. For a moment or two he could make out nothing in the gloomy loft, its wooden shutter tightly closed by the bar outside, the only light creeping in through the cracks in the wall. Then he saw the familiar undersized figure crouching in the corner like a trapped rat, a bulky object raised above his head, as if he were prepared to fight this strange intruder to the death. 'All right, yer little cripple,' he chortled. 'Don't piss yersen! Put that tin leg of yourn down. It's me, Teeth.'

'Teeth, Comrade Major,' Tinleg cried. 'It's Teeth come to rescue us!'

The Marshal raised himself from the straw where he had been crouching too, ready to do battle, heart missing a beat with joy, exactly in the same instant as the harsh voice in German below demanded, '*Na, was ist dann hier los?*'

Teeth's big head disappeared from the hole like a shot and for one long moment he hung there staring at the German who stood, braces dangling, in one hand a sheaf of newspaper, in the other a big pistol.

'*Heraus mit der Sprache. Was —*'

The big German's query ended in a yelp of pain, as Teeth lashed out his steel-tipped boot and caught him a glancing blow on the point of his chin. He smashed back against the wall, the pistol dropping from his hand. But he caught himself from falling altogether and in the very same moment as Teeth let go and fell to the floor, he dived forward. They crashed together and tumbled in a confused heap of flailing arms and legs on to the seat. Teeth reacted almost at once, but the German was quicker. He seized hold of the Russian's genitals and twisted hard. Teeth's scream of absolute agony was drowned fortunately by the sudden roar of a tank engine outside.

His steel teeth hanging out of his gaping mouth, now full of vomit, only half-conscious of what he was doing, Teeth rammed his elbow into the German's suddenly triumphant face. Something snapped harshly. Thick scarlet gobs of blood shot from the German's broken nose. He let go of his hold and reeled back against the wall.

Teeth sucked back his dental plates and swallowed the vomit. He grabbed hold of the German's throat in the very instant that he opened his mouth to scream. Desperately he hung on, while the big Fritz writhed back and forth, trying to break that terrible grip. What was he going to do with him? Any moment he might break loose and alert the sentry outside. Then he had it.

Exerting all his strength he forced the German down towards the open hatch. □

The German's eyes went wide with horror. He redoubled his frantic efforts to free himself. Gobs of blood splattered everywhere. Teeth used the last of his strength. Slowly he forced him down into the hole, the German fighting back the whole time. Suddenly he slipped and was inside. Teeth let go. The man clawed at the nauseating mess that smeared his bloody face, ready to scream. Teeth didn't give him a chance. Just as he opened his mouth to shout, human ordure dripping from his face, Teeth raised the butt of the man's own pistol and brought it down hard on the big shaven skull.

The German slipped deeper into the mess. Meaningless sounds came from his gaping mouth, as he started to sink with an awful squelching noise. Teeth didn't give him a chance. He smashed the butt down on his skull once more. Bone broke. Still the German fought back.

'Will you never die, you pig!' Teeth hissed at that terrible, contorted face, only centimetres from his own, as the ordure tried to suck him down. '*Never*?' He hit him again.

The German splashed forward. But his eyes were still open and he was conscious. The ordure bubbled with his dying gasps. Once more Teeth, shaking with fear, tension and rage, hit him. His face shot into the yellow liquid mess. His mouth filled which effectively blocked his scream of pain.

Teeth stared down in awe, pistol butt raised, ready to strike again, as the German's hand reached up, momentarily grasped the wooden seat, fingers jerking convulsively, before the spirit left him for good and the hand fell back. He was dead at last.

For what seemed an age, Teeth crouched there, body heaving with stifled chokes, as he vomited on to the man he had just killed, the tears streaming with passionate abandon down his grey face. In the end Tinleg's anxious whispered inquiry roused him from his stupor.

Five minutes later with the sentry outside the latrine dispatched quickly, efficiently and noiselessly by Tinleg's deadly little knife, they were on their way out of the camp, running blindly through the forest, followed by wild angry shots, heading for the Height and the new battle to come.

CHAPTER 5

'*Mein Gott, was eine Schweinerei!*' Manteuffel groaned, staring aghast at the dead bodies of the naked men and the nurses sprawled everywhere. 'For God's sake, somebody get a blanket and cover the women up at least.' He turned away, brushing aside his bodyguard as he walked outside into the clean air.

Already the gun batteries were rumbling past, swinging round the great smoking crater in the centre of the forest road, complete with wrecked gun-limber and the dead bodies of the horses still in their traces, the result of the explosion of one of the mines those swine's of Russians had planted there. Manteuffel fought to control himself, repressing the urge to vomit, and bringing up his binoculars focused them on the height to his front. It would be a tough nut to crack, he told himself, wondering, as he did so, why the Russians had not simply retreated across the Volga Canal. Why had they decided to stay on the German side of the waterway?

Naturally, on such steep slopes, the advantage would be on the side of the defender. A couple of well-sited machine-guns manned by determined gunners could well hold a whole battalion at bay.

He swung his binoculars round, staring at the height through the bright calibrated glass. On the slope facing the canal, as far as he could make out, the gradient was not so steep. He bit his bottom lip thoughtfully. Would the Russians attempt to defend it as strongly as the three slopes facing the Germans, he wondered. Psychologically speaking, they might be lulled into false confidence there, because, after all, they were opposite their own lines, from which naturally no attack would come.

Suddenly an idea began to dawn upon him. He lowered his glasses and swung round on his new aide, a pimply youth of eighteen with steel spectacles who bore a famous Prussian name like himself. 'Ask *Hauptsturmbannführer* Meier to report to me immediately, Gneisnau,' he barked.

'Meier, sir?' von Gneisnau exclaimed. 'But *Herr General*, he is of the SS!'

'Exactly.'

'But sir, I thought in the Seventh Armoured Division we had no truck with the SS. In the officers' mess they —'

'Gneisnau,' the General cut him short, 'you must not believe the gossip you hear in the officers' mess.'

'I know, sir, I don't,' von Gneisnau persisted with the innocent obstinacy of youth, 'but you've often said yourself, if I may be forgiven for saying so, that there are no gentlemen in the SS.'

General von Manteuffel smiled icily at the red-faced embarrassed young aide, whose great ancestor had once restored a defeated Prussian army to its old glory. 'For the task of dealing with those Russian animals who did that back there, Gneisnau, I don't want gentlemen. I want killers! Now cut along and get me Meier!'

Hauptsturmbannführer Meier, burly barrel-chested Bavarian, who had come from Dachau Concentration Camp to take charge of the company of the SS *Totenkopf* currently attached to the 7th Panzer Division for intensive training under battlefield conditions in tank warfare, smiled happily to himself as he walked away from the general half an hour later.

In spite of his gross, bully-boy appearance, Meier was no fool. He knew exactly why von Manteuffel had picked him and his SS men for the first assault on the Ivans. The SS were prepared to take heavier casualties than the ordinary *Wehrmacht* stubble-hopper would. But it wasn't only that. Von Manteuffel had not said so in so many words, but his underlying motive in giving the mission to the SS was clear enough: after the rape and murder of the nurses, the little snob of a general wanted no survivors. The SS could be relied upon to slaughter the Popovs on that hill to the very last man.

'Assignment, *Hauptsturm*?' Peters, his second-in-command, a tall white-blond from Schleswig-Holstein, asked eagerly as he strode into the SS company's camp. 'Hopefully. The boys are getting corns on their keesters sitting around here and seeing no action.'

Meier grinned at him. Wordlessly he held out his hand.

Walters grinned back and handed him his own "flat-man". He knew they'd got a mission.

Meier uncorked the flat bottle of corn *schnapps* and tilting back his head took a mighty slug of it. He choked, shuddered and smiled, his broad peasant face suddenly dark red. 'Herr Peters,' he said, 'we have indeed got an assignment. We're gonna toast the eggs off'n some Popovs.'

Peters' long Nordic face lit up. 'The flame-throwers?'

'The flame-throwers!' Meier echoed.

'Shit!... Now that is what I call a real assignment.' Peters swung round and shouted, just as the first German battery opened up on Height 444, 'All right, you bunch of green-assed wet tails, on your feet... *We're going in...*'

But the troopers of the SS *Totenkopf* were not the only elite troops massing for the attack that late afternoon. On the other side of the canal, the cadets of the Stalin Scholars Corps were also preparing for their baptism of blood. Watched by anxious NCOs, tugging at their smart uniforms, setting their helmets squarely as regulations prescribed on their shaven skulls, the young fanatics, each one of them a member of the *Kolsomol* they formed their assault lines.

Colonel Hardt, as firm and unyielding as his German name, their commandant, had no eyes for the waterway they were to attack. His gaze was fixed on his young men, checking if their lines were straight, their uniform buttons fastened and their cotton gloves were still white. Satisfied, he swept back the huge curving moustache that he affected in the style of the old Red Army cavalry officer, and bellowed in that tremendous voice of his which was reputed by awed cadets to carry well over a kilometre, '*Adjutant!*'

'Colonel Commandant?'

'Bring up the band.'

The young adjutant swallowed hard. *The band!* He shook his head. They were all crazy, the commandant and the whole Corps of Cadets. He shrugged and called to the bandmaster, dressed in gala uniform, complete with shining sword, 'Bandmaster, bring up the band.'

Dutifully the resplendent bandmaster raised his baton. 'In step, no music, the band will — *advance*,' he cried above the roar of the bombardment on the other side of the canal.

Heavy-footed and pompous somehow, eight abreast, their instruments gleaming in the last rays of the weak winter sun, the band advanced to come to a halt at the side of the Stalin Scholars drawn up in rigid lines under the cover of the trees.

Colonel Hardt nodded his approval. Drill was improving in general, he told himself, and it was drill that made soldiers, not all this new-fangled military science nonsense. Turning, he crunched across the hard scuffed snow to where Natasha, his big white mare, was waiting motionlessly, as unaffected by the German fire as he himself. Effortlessly he swung himself on to the horse's back and patted her neck in approval. An instant later he drew his gleaming silver sabre and rested it across his right shoulder. Now he sat there, rigid-backed and with that look on his face that had turned many a cadet's knees to water, waiting for darkness to fall. There was silence now save for the rumble of the guns.

The stage was set. The actors were in place. The drama could commence!

CHAPTER 6

'Dig *in ... dig in!*'

Furiously a red-faced Colonel Katukov kicked and lashed out at his still drunken men, as they collapsed on the top of the height, chests heaving, breath coming in leathern-lunged gasps, the shells dropping everywhere unheeded in their exhaustion. 'Come on, on your feet, you drunken swine ... or you Gulag scum won't live to see another dawn!'

'Dig *in, men... Dig in!*'

Now the surviving officers and men, roused out of their lethargy by Katukov's fury, staggered from man to man, pulling each to his feet and thrusting a bayonet or his own entrenching tool into his hand so that the exhausted Gulag rat could begin digging in.

The Marshal wiped the sweat off his brow with the back of his hand and ignoring the shells, took stock of their position. Katukov, or whoever had selected the place, had picked well. Their front opposite the Fritzes was steep and un-wooded, offering an excellent field of fire; the enemy would take terrible losses if they attempted to attack from there. He turned and faced their rear, as yet only half aware of the change in the character of the falling shells. Beyond the canal, their own positions were shrouded in mist and smoke. Obviously the Red Army frontline troops were burning smoke-pots to hide the massing of the shock battalions for the coming offensive; it was standard operating procedure. The rear slope of Height 444 was as yet, however, clear. The Marshal wrinkled his big nose at what he saw there.

The gradient was certainly not half as steep as the other slopes; in addition it was well wooded and would offer ample cover for attacking infantry until they reached virtually the top of Height 444. It was, in short, the natural approach for any attacker; but, on the other hand, it *was* covered from their own positions across the canal — that was, as long as daylight revealed the attacking troops to their own men dug in over there. The Marshal made a sudden decision. In the same instant he became aware that at last the enemy was no longer pumping high explosive shells at them; now the HE was mixed with smoke that was already beginning to drift across the summit and obscure their positions. 'Teeth,' he called, 'and you, Tinleg, move those leaden butts of yourn. Get a section with a heavy M.G. up here — at the double!'

'At the double, Comrade Major!' Teeth yelled back dutifully, and forgetting his exhaustion after the long, panic-stricken run through the forest, he started to cry out orders. Seconds later, the machine-gun section, pulling their ancient wheeled machine-gun behind them, were doubling through the ever-increasing brown fog to the still smoking shell-hole overlooking the rear slope.

Cautiously, very cautiously, crouched low in their rubber dinghies, Meier's *Totenkopf* troopers paddled ever closer to the rear slope of Height 444, keeping near to their own bank, alert eyes fixed on the billowing smoke to their front anxiously. Now they were sitting ducks if the smoke screen chanced to clear and reveal their presence a matter of metres away from the Popov positions.

But luck was on their side. Cloaked in the brown fog they touched the bank right under the height in the very same instant as Manteuffel's mortars tore apart the air somewhere above them. 'Right on time, Peters,' Meier hissed to his second-in-command.

'The Army is not all bad,' the tall North German hissed back. 'Occasionally they manage to get some simple thing right.' □

Hauptsturmbannführer Meier grinned and then, as dinghy after dinghy started to nudge against the bank, concentrated on getting his men unloaded.

Finally the task was completed, while Manteuffel's mortarmen plastered the other side of the canal, which was still shrouded in the smoke screen, obstructing the bold men landing right under their very noses.

Meier checked his little force, one hundred men against an estimated Popov battalion dug in above them somewhere on the summit of Height 444.

Peters read his company commander's mind. 'We're the SS, *Hauptsturm*,' he said proudly. 'One good wet fart of one of us is good enough to make ten Ivans turn up their toes and join old Father Marx in whatever paradise that particular Jew has picked for himself.'

'Well, I don't know about that, Peters. But this little baby,' he patted the round container on the back of the nearest flame-thrower operator affectionately, 'is going to equal the odds some.'

'They'll fry their Bolshy blubber for them all right,' Peters agreed enthusiastically.

Meier eyed his men. They were all ready, each one of the operators covered by four riflemen. He was satisfied. Even without orders, his elite had known what to do. They did not wear the silver skull-and-crossbones and the hard cruel SS runes for nothing. He pumped his right fist up and down three times: the infantry signal for advance.

'*Vorwärts!*' Peters ordered, his long face set in a smile of wolfish pleasure at the thought of the great killing to come soon.

Well-spaced out, they filtered into the snow-heavy trees. One minute later they had vanished completely, swallowed up by the firs, leaving behind their slowly sinking dinghies. As always there would be no retreat for the SS. For them the motto was: *fight or die!*

Colonel Hardt, his back as straight as a ramrod, frowned at the big Cossack on his shaggy untidy pony, its flanks gleaming with sweat after the hard gallop. He took his time, as befitted the feared commandant of Stalin Scholars, running his eagle eye up and down the Cossack's shabby blouse and unpolished equipment before finally deigning to ask the courier, 'What did you say the General ordered, soldier?'

The big Cossack doffed his fur hat once more in the style of the old Tsarist Army when a Cossack reported to an officer. 'The Comrade General says that the Comrade Colonel should attack forthwith — *respectfully!* The Comrade General states that the Fr — er, the enemy is massing himself for an attack — *respectfully!* The Comrade Colonel is urged to take immediate counterattack — *respectfully!*' The Cossack replaced his fur hat on his jet-black curls and waited obediently for the Colonel's reply.

Hardt stared at the brown whirling fog in front of him, which now completely covered the canal. Martinet and parade-ground soldier that he was, Hardt still had been a fighting man once and his experience told him that the activities of the enemy indicated more that *they* feared an attack than that they were going to attack themselves. Still, he had never disobeyed an order in his whole life. It was a basic truth that he drummed into his cadets right from the start: 'An order is an order, not to be considered, discussed, interpreted, but to be executed — *at once!*'

'*Horoscho!*' he exclaimed. 'Tell the Comrade General that the Stalin Scholars will advance *now!*'

'Thank you, Comrade Colonel,' the Cossack yelled above the whine of the exploding mortar shells. Viciously he slashed his knout across the shining rump of his animal and was away at the gallop, as if the devil himself were after him.

'Cossacks,' the colonel told himself scornfully, 'they're all the same. Lots of prancing and wheeling and showing off for the wenches, but when it comes to real fighting, they are off as quickly as their horses can carry them!' Then he dismissed the courier and, wheeling Natasha, trotted back slowly to where the Scholars waited in rigid lines.

He reined in the mare and stared from left to right along their ranks. They were wet-eared boys, he had to admit that, and there were pale faces enough among their ranks, yet if they were scared, they were not showing it otherwise. Green and inexperienced as they were, he knew he could rely upon them.

He raised his voice above the racket. 'Cadets,' he cried, 'this is the first time. You will fight and not run away. If necessary you will die rather than that.' He raised himself in his stirrups and bellowed, '*Long live Comrade Stalin!*'

'*Long live Comrade Stalin!*' The hoarse cheer rose from a thousand young throats.

'Long live Russia and the Corps of Cadets!'

Again the cheer was echoed mightily.

'And remember — keep a tight arsehole, boys,' Colonel Hardt said, relaxing a moment, remembering his own reaction as a fifteen-year-old at his first battle in another war.

The boys in the front rank, whatever they might have been feeling at that particular moment, returned his grin.

Colonel Hardt's face hardened again. 'Bandmaster,' he cried, 'are you deaf, man?'

'At your command, Comrade Colonel!' the fat music-master cried in a red-faced fluster, as he doubled forward and looked up at the man on the horse.

'A march — a smart, lively march. We advance!'

'At your command. Have you —'

But Hardt was already spurring Natasha forward so that he was in the centre front. Behind him the adjutant followed, wishing that he was back in Moscow with the girls and the pink Crimean champagne instead of following this old fool who would lead him and the rest to a certain death because he had never disobeyed an order, however stupid, in his whole life. Without looking back, Hardt judged when the adjutant was in position too, then he called, 'Corps of Cadets — *attention*!' A thousand pairs of feet stamped down on the hard snow.

'Corps of Cadets — *dress ranks*!'

He waited until they had finished shuffling their feet and having dressed their ranks so that they stood in immaculately straight lines, eyes front again, then he gave his final order, raising himself in his stirrups and expanding his chest to its full capacity. 'Corps of Cadets — AD-VANCE!'

As one the thousand Stalin Scholars, fanatical, eager for glory and an early death, stepped forward, bayonets flashing as they brought them to the front, highly polished boots crunching across the frozen snow.

The huge drummer struck his big drum. Its hollow boom was the signal for the rest of the band. Brass blared, trumpets sounded, and to the steady, almost ominous thump-thump of the drum, the musicians started to accompany the youths to their appointment with death.

'Well, I'll go and piss in my boot!' the soldier crouched in his rifle pit on the edge of the canal exclaimed in awe. 'Do you hear that? The Ivans have brought up a band.'

Manteuffel raised his binoculars. The smoke screen was beginning to clear slowly now. It had served its purpose. Meier's men were safely landed and were in position on the height now. Hurriedly he focused them, trying to penetrate the swirling fog. His mouth dropped open stupidly.

Advancing towards the opposite bank, there were three long lines of infantry, accompanied by a band in gala uniform, at their head two officers on white chargers, 'Impossible, Gneisnau,' he breathed. 'Absolutely impossible!'

Gneisnau lowered his own glasses. 'But *Herr General*, it's like something out of the eighteenth century… The way Old Fritz fought the Seven Years War. I mean…' Words failed the bespectacled youth and he stood there on the bank, mouth open stupidly, as the blare of the enemy brass band grew ever louder and, along the German line, gunners cocked their pieces and swung up their rifles to face the advancing Russians.

Manteuffel did not react for a moment. As an eighteen-year-old officer-cadet at the Battle of Tannenberg in 1914 he had seen the Russians advance like this once before, urged on by Cossacks wielding whips to their backs, to be mown down by their thousands, but still coming on until there were great walls of Russian dead in front of the Imperial Guards' positions. But that had been nearly a quarter of a century before. Surely in the middle of a total war, the Russians would not attempt another attack of that kind, which could only result in a massacre?

He focused his glasses once more, as if to reassure himself that what he had seen was not true. But it was.

Three dead-straight lines of infantry advanced towards them, bayonets tucked under their right arms, as if they were taking part in the October Revolution parade on Red Square, two ramrod-stiff officers trotting easily at their front, sabres rested on their shoulders.

He let the binoculars drop by the strap and groaned, touching his forehead, as if his head had suddenly begun to ache.

'What are we going to do, sir?' Gneisnau asked, abruptly recovering his powers of speech, but his awed gaze still fixed on the Russians.

'Do? Massacre the poor young fools,' Manteuffel groaned. 'That's what we're going to do, Gneisnau!'

Meier thrust back his battered peak-cap adorned with the tarnished silver skull-and-crossbones badge and wiped his sweating forehead. All around him his gasping men, bent under their heavy equipment, leaned against the trees and rested, while Peters conferred with the CO.

'It'll be as easy as falling off a log, sir,' Peters said confidently. 'I got within twenty metres of their positions without being spotted. I could see everything.'

'What's their strength?' Meier asked, frowning a little with bewilderment at the sound of what seemed *Marsch-musik* somewhere to their rear.

'Not much that I could see, anyway, facing us. About a section of rifle-men dug in — and one of those M.G.s of theirs. You know the things, *Hauptsturm*, mounted on wheels with a little metal shield.' He laughed easily. 'Looks as if they might have pulled it out of some museum.'

Meier absorbed the information, mentally making his dispositions. Like most SS officers he despised the Popovs as fourth, even fifth-class soldiers for the most part. He had seen them run by the thousand as soon as they had crossed the River Bug into Russia the previous June. All the same he had a healthy respect for the Russian's ability to stand terrible punishment once he was well dug in and commanded by capable officers; and he knew that he could not afford, with the small number of men at his disposal, to get bogged down.

'All right, Peters, now this is what we will do...'

Now the advancing Russians were almost at the edge of the canal. As yet not a shot had been fired at them by the waiting Germans. It was almost as if they were mesmerized into inactivity by the sight of these men advancing to certain death.

'Halt!'

The cry floated across the canal and the waiting infantry watched open-mouthed as the young men on the opposite side came to an abrupt stop at the command of the man mounted on the white mare.

Von Manteuffel shook his head, as if he could not believe the evidence of his own eyes.

The band stopped playing suddenly. Slowly, deliberately, the man on the leading horse dismounted, as if challenging the unseen Germans to shoot him. Transfixed, the men lying in the firing pits watched him as he swung round with a flourish and eyed the boys standing there stiffly at attention. Seemingly satisfied with what he saw, he turned to his front again and faced the canal.

'Corps of Cadets will advance — *at the double!*... DOUBLE!'

Pointing his sabre at the other side, the officer ran forward, followed by his men, a great hoarse cry rising from their young throats, as they pointed their bayonets towards the enemy. They hit the water with a series of huge splashes and plunged on.

After what seemed an age, the Germans finally woke up to their danger. Officers blew their alarm whistles, NCOs bellowed orders and the line broke into a ragged volley of fire. Purple flame stabbed the gloom as the machine-guns started to chatter lethally a moment later. Desperately the Stalin Scholars came on, taking casualties by the score, threshing and dying in the abruptly wild water, that already was beginning to turn red with their blood.

Manteuffel turned his head away momentarily, sickened by this senseless slaughter of the youthful idealists dying and drowning in the canal. This wasn't war; it was murder!

'Look out, sir!' Gneisnau at his side called urgently. He spun round.

A tall Russian with a heavy old-fashioned cavalry moustache, his once immaculate uniform now soaked, was rushing at him up the bank, his silver sabre raised.

Manteuffel reacted instinctively, while Gneisnau stood immobile at his side, as if paralysed. His hand flashed to his holster. He pulled out his pistol and fired from the hip without aiming. The Russian staggered but continued running for a moment so that Manteuffel thought he had missed. But the growing red patch on his breast told him he hadn't. The Russian staggered. The sabre dropped from his nerveless fingers. He attempted to clutch his chest, failed and pitched forward on to the snow.

The death of Colonel Hardt took the heart out of the cadets. Those who had survived the crossing and were beginning to clamber up the body-littered bank started to retreat, firing as they backed off to the water, taking casualties all the time, until in the end a sickened Manteuffel called, 'Cease firing ... cease firing, let the poor fools go!'

The firing died away to allow the survivors to swim and wade back the way they had come to where the band crouched stupidly, staring at the slaughter with uncomprehending eyes.

Wearily, shoulders bowed as if burdened by a great weight, the little general crossed to where the Russian officer lay. He turned him over with the toe of his boot. He was dead. They were all dead on this side of the canal. For what purpose? Nothing.

'What now, sir?' Gneisnau asked in a little voice, awed by the slaughter all around.

'Now?' Manteuffel echoed, as if he were having difficulty in understanding the question.

'Yessir. Will they come again, sir?'

Manteuffel shook his head several times like a person trying to wake from a deep, deep sleep. 'Oh yes, they'll come again all right, Gneisnau. This is just the start.' He inclined his head towards the smoke-shrouded summit of Height 444. 'Those up there are just the vanguard. They'll come again and by God, if they are as bold and brave as these' — he looked at the dead young men all around, sprawled in the extravagant postures of the violently done-to-death — 'then heaven help Germany...'

CHAPTER 7

In spite of the freezing cold, the flies had appeared somehow or other. Now they fed on the dead sprawled in the shell-craters which dotted the summit everywhere. They were fat, dark-blue, slow objects which looked like grapes on wings as they buzzed from corpse to corpse amid the shattered ground, giving off the sweet stench of carrion. Occasionally the corpses groaned softly and twitched, as if they were alive and irritated by the importuning of the flies. But the Marshal knew that wasn't the case. It was the imprisoned gases in their swollen, bloated stomachs that gave off the noise and made them move. They were dead all right.

For what, he wondered gloomily, as he squatted in his hole, trying to doze a little before the next bombardment. For a feature on the map, which did not even have a name. *Height 444*! Would that number ever conjure up to anyone else the cowardice and daring, the suffering, the fear, the agony of the men who would fight and die here?

He doubted it. He took his gaze off the body of the young officer of Intelligence who had been their guide. Now he lay dead, the fat blue flies feeding on the gory mess of his shattered skull. Instead he gazed at the white waste beyond the shell-craters, over which they would come, now the attack across the canal had been beaten off. He tried to concentrate on the military problem, but couldn't somehow. He knew the mood he was in, a mixture of apathetic depression and inability to concentrate, was a result of too much action and too little sleep. He knew, too, it was a dangerous mood to be in. When it possessed a soldier, especially if he were responsible for other men's lives, he could make mistakes that were fatal.

'A drink, Comrade Major?'

The educated voice woke him from his reverie with a start. He turned. It was Vulf, the inevitable bottle in his hand outstretched in his direction.

He took it, automatically wiped the neck with a dirty hand and drank a deep draught of the fiery liquid. He shook and gasped for breath. 'Thanks, Vulf,' he said thickly, handing it back to the grinning young intellectual as he squatted there in the snow, looking down into the Marshal's hole. 'And you'd better get in here before some nasty Fritz sharpshooter lets some air into the back of your head.'

Vulf took a drink himself first before saying, 'Thanks for the good advice, Major, but I'm a fatalist. What will be, will be. You cannot stop fate.'

'Perhaps.'

'It is as good a philosophy as any, fatalism,' Vulf said mildly, staring at the Marshal from behind those thick-lensed spectacles of his owlishly. 'It can even make a devout coward like me somewhat brave, and it is the ideal creed for us Russians.'

'Why particularly the Russians?' the Marshal asked without too much interest, his mind on other things.

'Throughout our existence as a race we have never been able to change our fate. It has been determined for us by a series of Norsemen, Tartars, Mongols, Cossacks, Tsars and the like. We did manage — *just once* — to attempt to take our fate in our own hands, in 1917, if you recall, and what did we get?' He laughed a little bitterly. 'We got Stalin! So why should we worry about the course of events? Let them take care of themselves.

We may not be happy about them, but at least we will not be actively unhappy.'

The Marshal looked at him curiously. 'Vulf, how in God's name did you survive for so long in Moscow with views like that? No, don't attempt to answer. I don't agree with you. You can buck fate; at least, a man should try.'

Vulf rose to his feet once more, a mocking smile on his clever face. 'Fate, my dear Major, is Colonel Katukov. As long as he is — er,' he hesitated the merest fraction of a second, but it sufficed to inform the Marshal that Vulf knew of the officers' plan to get rid of the CO, 'around, we are powerless to buck fate, as you put it.' With that he was gone.

The Marshal watched him go unhurriedly, telling himself that Vulf's concept of fatalism certainly made him unafraid; he walked back to his post as if he were a man of leisure taking a stroll through a Moscow park in peacetime. Then he considered the other man's words. Katukov was indeed the stumbling block. But what would they do once they had eradicated him and could exercise their own free will? They would have killed the chief jailer well enough, but they would still be inside the jail.

Before he had time to consider that familiar and frustrating problem, Teeth's voice roared, '*Income mail*... Hit the dirt, Gulag swine... Hit th —'

The rest of his warning was drowned by the first salvo of the new barrage thundering down and making the very earth shimmy under their impact.

Obediently the Marshal hit the dirt.

'I hope those shitty followers of Saint Barbara have been keeping their hands off the sauce for once,' Peters roared over the new thunder of the guns. 'One slip and we're going to have a very bad headache.'

Meier grinned back at his second-in-command. 'We might be in luck this time, Peters,' he said easily and paused for a moment in the ascent. Above, the summit was again ringed with thick brown smoke, disturbed at regular intervals by a flash of flame as yet another shell struck home.

It had been a gruelling slog, especially as the Popovs might well have spotted them at any time. Now they were in dead ground and in the position Meier had picked for launching his attack. Everything was going as planned.

'There'll be tin in this one, *Hauptsturm*,' Peters said. 'I can feel it in my brittle bones.'

'Yes, War Service Cross, third class,' Meier replied scornfully. 'Did you ever hear of a *Wehrmacht* general recommending an SS man for a decoration? Come on, let's get this show on the road.'

He turned to the flame-throwers, looking apprehensive now that the action was going to begin. Their position was indeed unenviable. One bullet into the pack of fuel on their shoulders and they would go up like a torch. 'I know what you boys are feeling like,' he said. 'But we'll look after you. The Popovs won't get within sniffing distance of you. Your comrades, the riflemen, will take care of that.' He turned his attention to the riflemen, knowing that they did not like the task of defending the flame-thrower operators. If the pack exploded, they'd burn too if they were close enough. 'Now, I'm warning you,' he said grimly. 'I'll have the eggs off anyone of you — with a blunt razorblade — if he gets more than five metres away from his operator. If the Popov's don't get you, I *will*. *Klar*?'

'*Klar*,' they answered uneasily.

He grinned. 'Don't sound so enthusiastic. Besides the Popovs'll cream their skivvies the moment they see the flame-throwers. They always do. Believe you me, they'll be falling over themselves to surrender, once we've tickled 'em up with a bit of fire.'

But for once *Hauptsturmbannführer* Manfred Meier was wrong, very wrong.

It was by chance that Colonel Katukov spotted the Germans creeping up on the summit position. Katukov was a private man in all things. Whereas any other of his soldiers would have performed his natural functions in front of his comrades, using the bottom of his slit trench or an empty shell case to carry them out, Katukov could not have stood that. He had to be alone. Thus it was that during a slight lull in the enemy bombardment, he doubled out of the slit trench he shared with a now grinning Vulf to the nearest shell crater on the edge of the Gulag rats' perimeter to satisfy a pressing need.

Squatting there, keeping his head well down, for it would not be long, he knew, before the next salvo of Fascist shells would come winging their way bearing their lethal load, he saw the first of the all too familiar coal-scuttle helmets come slowly into view.

His own needs were forgotten immediately. Under the cover of the bombardment, the Fascists had penetrated to within fifty metres of their position. Swiftly he hauled up his trousers and grabbed for his pistol.

Hastily he levelled it at the first cautious figure, apparently a Fritz officer as he raised his arm to wave at the rest to follow him. Abruptly his heart missed a beat. Behind him another soldier raised himself to reveal that terrifying pack on his shoulders. *Flame-thrower!*

By a sheer effort of naked will-power Katukov forced himself to take aim. He squeezed the trigger. There was a howl of pain and Peters went crashing and tumbling down the slope and Colonel Katukov was running back to the Russian positions for all his life was worth, with that terrifying all-consuming flame roaring after him.

CHAPTER 8

The first skirmish-line broke within five minutes. The survivors, living torches all of them, ran screaming to the rear, trailing blue flame after them, leaving behind them in rifle-pits indescribable, charred hunks of meat which had once been men.

Yelling the triumphant battle-cry of the SS, '*All for Germany!*' the attackers lumbered forward, each group of riflemen packed in around the flame-thrower operator so that it was virtually impossible to knock him out.

Piotr, face blackened and scorched, crazy with rage at what had happened to his company, refused to withdraw. Standing there on the ridge, he pumped shot after shot from his revolver into the advancing Germans.

Boldin and Katukov, cowering in a shell-hole some fifty metres away, watched awestruck as that terrible flame came closer and closer to the one-armed officer. Boldin flung a stick-grenade at the nearest operator. It exploded harmlessly, too short. He groaned as that long tongue of greedy flame reached out like the tongue of some predatory monster searching blindly for its petrified prey. Even at that distance a horrified Boldin could feel his hair begin to singe, as that tremendous heat engulfed them. 'RUN ... RUN, PIOTR!' he screamed desperately above the roar of flame.

Piotr remained where he was, firing, firing, his face glowing a dull red as the flame was reflected on its sweat-lathered skin. Then it caught him, sweeping up his body, submerging him in that cruel, all-consuming, terrible flame. He sank into it, his already blackened, petrified claws reaching upwards, as if he were climbing an invisible ladder, and disappeared for a moment while the flame did its deadly work.

The flame swept back with a great hush, leaving behind it a charred pigmy in the steaming burning puddle of blue fluid, Piotr's body reduced by that searing flame to half its original size.

Boldin fought back the bile that rose sickeningly into his throat, his nostrils full of the stench of burnt flesh. Next to him Katukov gasped for air, his mouth open like a stranded fish in its death throes. Summoning up the last of his strength, knowing that the whole line would run if the Germans weren't stopped now, Boldin attempted to rise, tugging at his pistol holster.

Katukov reacted more quickly. 'Get down,' he commanded and pushed Boldin to one side.

The flame-thrower operator fired again. The fire wrapped itself around their hiding place. Boldin choked for breath as the flame drew the oxygen forcibly from his lungs. For an instant, the very soil in front of him glowed. Then the flame had gone and Katukov, the slugs cutting the air all around him unheeded, was on his feet, his signal pistol raised as if he were standing on some peacetime firing range. He took careful aim.

The signal flare hit the flame-thrower operator squarely on his chest. Katukov could see the puff of smoke on impact quite clearly. For a moment nothing happened. Then the flare exploded, tearing a great ragged hole in the man's chest and followed a moment later by the whoosh of the fuel tank on his back exploding, scattering furiously burning oil over the riflemen. In an instant all was screaming chaos, with riflemen dropping their rifles in their fear, scattering for cover, attempting to beat out the flames leaping up from their burning uniforms with hands that were on fire themselves, while on the ground the tube of the flamethrower gasped and died like some strange rubber snake.

Boldin could not speak for what seemed a long time. Below the Germans ran for cover, the steam gone out of their attack for a while, then as the defenders rallied and□ the first ragged volley crashed home, he gasped, 'You saved us, Colonel … the Gulag rats, *you saved us*!'

Katukov licked cracked, parched lips. 'You … you are the only command I've got. You're not as bad soldiers as I thought you were.'

In spite of their desperate position, Boldin stared at Colonel Katukov in amazement. In the hard harsh face of that remote man, there was something akin to pride. '*Boshe moi*,' he told himself, 'he's proud of us!'

Meier looked around at the faces of his men as they crouched among the rocks, while the Popov slugs whined off them everywhere. His cocky confident smile had vanished now, and his men no longer looked as sure of victory as they had been at the outset of the attack. That nasty business with the flame-thrower operator, which had cost not only his life but that of four riflemen, had upset them. He knew they needed pepping up.

'Now listen,' he urged, 'regard it as a bit of bad luck. As they say, you can't make a shitting omelette without cracking eggs. This time we don't give them a chance. We hit them in one small sector with all we've got. Where?' Meier answered his own question. 'The flank. We'll work our way round there.' He indicated the snow-covered ridge to their right. 'Riflemen first, with the operators coming up twenty metres to the rear. You see, you'll be perfectly safe until the time comes to hit them.'

He grinned at the still shaken operators, his teeth a gleaming white against his dirty, tough Bavarian face.

'*Jesusmaria, josepf!* It'll be simple, once we've located the furthest extent of their flank over there, we'll come in with massed flame-throwers. We'll roll 'em — just like that!' He snapped his thumb and forefinger together triumphantly. 'Believe you me, comrades, it'll be a walkover.' His grin vanished. 'All right, out the scouts!' he ordered. 'Get some pepper in your arses now. Let's go!'

But not only the SS captain was making fresh plans at that moment; the Gulag rats were too.

Just in front of the hole in which Katukov, Boldin and Vulf crouched, Teeth was sawing furiously at the nose of a 9mm slug, while Tinleg anxiously watched the shattered front for any sign of fresh German movement. 'Dum-dum,' Teeth explained as he gouged a line crosswise with the aid of an abandoned bayonet. 'The Tommies used them against us in the Revolution. Said the dum-dum bullet should only be fired against native troops — and Bolsheviks, because we didn't go on our shitting bony knees like they did and pray to the Big Uncle up there.' He indicated the leaden, snow-heavy sky with the point of the bayonet.

'But what's so special about it, Teeth?' Tinleg asked puzzled, but not taking his eyes off the front and those terribly mutilated charred bodies.

'Yer normal slug at close range goes right through the human body. Son-of-a-whore, I've seen men keeping on running after being hit because they didn't even know that they had been. With a dum-dum, it's a lot different. It bursts when it hits. It'll stop a half-a-ton of bull — *dead!* And that's what we want, now. We want to stop those Fritz flame-thrower operators at a nice safe distance, Tinleg.'

Tinleg shivered visibly. 'That you can say again, Teeth. Stop them at a nice safe distance, *and how!*'

The problem of distance was one that occupied the officers behind the two NCOs at that moment, too. 'Our only course is to withdraw, Boldin,' Katukov was saying. 'Give ourselves some depth so that we can pick off the operators before they can get within firing distance. My guess is that their range is about seventy metres. All right, we'll pull back one hundred and fifty. Yes, that is about it. We'll be just on the edge of the summit at that distance.'

'But, Comrade Colonel,' Boldin protested, 'you are an experienced soldier. You know the manoeuvre you are suggesting is one of the most difficult, even with men who are not exhausted like our men are. Breaking off action at close quarters could easily lead to a rout. Once they start running, especially with those terrible flamethrowers, there is no knowing when they'll stop.'

'I know, I know,' Katukov said hastily, knowing that they had no time to lose. 'But we won't all withdraw. We'll leave some men behind to cover us.'

'What?' Boldin exploded. 'Who do you expect to sacrifice themselves for us?'

Vulf smiled amused at the look of sheer outrage on the Major's tough face. As always he was amused by ideals and integrity. Indeed everything amused him, especially human virtue; at least he hoped it did. It was the only way he had managed not to go crazy in thirty-odd years of living in the 'Socialist Paradise'. He waited eagerly to hear what the colonel's reaction would be.

'Look, Boldin,' Katukov said urgently. 'We haven't got the time to debate this thing in detail. I know what you feel about those Gulag rats of yours. I know, too, what you feel about me — I'm not blind. But don't you be either! All your Gulag rats are not heroes, motivated by what you would regard as noble feelings, who have been imprisoned falsely by a corrupt oppressive system. No, Boldin! There are *real* rats among them, murderers, pimps, homosexuals, whoremasters, thieves, oh, you know what I'm talking about all right, Major. You know better than I do because you put them in one particular company — *shunting the shit*, they used to call it when I was a young officer.'

Boldin flashed a bitter look at Vulf; instinctively he knew where Katukov had his information from. 'All right, get on with it.'

'I will,' Katukov replied hastily, already aware of the movement on the fascist side of the line. 'Sacrifice the worst, what's left of Major Piotr's Company, to save the — er — *best.*'

Vulf's grin broadened. Katukov had choked on the word, twisting his head to one side, as if his collar were too tight and strangling him. □

'Am I God?' Boldin asked, knowing that Katukov was right.

'No. Just a realist, who knows that in war hard decisions have to be made. Well?'

Boldin hesitated only for a fraction of a second. '*Horoscho!*' he snapped, face hard and set. 'We'll do as you say, Comrade Colonel. But how are we going to keep those — rats — of yours in the line when the rest of us start to pull back, eh?'

Katukov's face relaxed momentarily into a mocking smile. 'Because my dear Boldin, one of us is going to stay behind with that machine-gun and make them hold the line... We might even be acclaimed as a hero later — posthumously, of course.'

Before Boldin could react, Colonel Katukov reached into the pocket of his ripped, blackened breeches and brought out a *kopek*. He balanced it on his thumbnail. 'What's it going to be, Boldin? ... number or star?'

Boldin, hesitated, not because he was afraid for his own life; that was forfeit sooner or later anyway, if not today, then tomorrow. Suddenly, however, he saw that if Katukov lost and were forced to stay behind, all their problems would be solved. If he were in sole charge, he could order a withdrawal through the Fritz lines and if they didn't make it back to the other side of the canal, then he could surrender. At least the Gulag rats might have a fighting chance of survival in the Fritz POW camps. 'All right, Katukov,' he said hoarsely, while the noises from the Germans grew louder and Vulf watched fascinated, as if he were viewing some particularly unusual experiment, 'toss!'

Katukov tossed the coin. 'Call!' he commanded.

'Star,' Boldin called, as Katukov caught the falling *kopek* neatly and held it out for Boldin to view, a mocking grin on his face. It was lying there with the red star upwards; Boldin had won. Katukov dropped the little brass coin. 'All right, Major Boldin, get moving. Time is running out fast...'

CHAPTER 9

An eerie nervous silence hung over the embattled summit now. The only sound to disturb it was the rumble of the Red Army's artillery on the other side across the canal. There they were preparing for a new attack after the disastrous failure of the Stalin Scholars. But the occasional monumental crashes of the heavies and the bass chatter of the heavy machine-guns meant nothing to the waiting men; they knew they would probably not survive to see the new attack.

Boldin had no ears for the sounds, nor eyes for anything but the lone figure sprawled thirty metres to his front, body twisted to the right of the machine-gun, feet spread at the regulation forty-five-degree angle. To the very last Colonel Katukov was a stickler for rules and regulations; he might well have been lying there on some peacetime range.

Before the lone machine-gunner lay what was left of Number One Company and even at that distance, Boldin could smell their fear, as the unseen Germans, armed with those terrible weapons of theirs, crept ever closer to their hilltop position. Now their systems would be pumped full of adrenalin, making their hearts beat furiously and their limbs tremble uncontrollably like those of epileptics. In a matter of minutes, Boldin knew instinctively, they would break, spring from their shallow holes, and rush the lone machine-gunner, who forced them, now, against every known human feeling to hold their positions in the face of that inhuman threat.

'Let us go, shit-eater!' the animal cry of pleading despair rose from the front line. 'Everyone here hates your rotten sadistic guts,' the inhuman howl continued, '*let us go… For God's sake, before it's too late!*'

Boldin, the small hairs at the nape of his neck standing erect with fear and dread at that awful cry for deliverance before it was too late, saw Katukov's shoulders hunch as if he had tightened his hold on his gun, ready to fire now.

'Don't our lives mean a fucking thing to you?' the animal voice screamed. 'Don't they?'

'Well, Comrade Major, don't they?' a soft educated voice asked at Boldin's side.

He turned slowly, knowing instinctively who had spoken.

'There's still time to run … and he's not in a position to stop us anymore.'

There was neither fear nor urgency on Vulf's face, just curiosity, as if the situation on hand did not interest him, only Boldin's reaction. He stared at the older man as he might have at some laboratory animal being subjected to a Pavlovian experiment.

'*Please*,' that unknown animal voice from Number One Company howled, 'please, we can hear the Fritzes. They're just to our right., *Please…*' The anger had gone now, to be replaced by sheer naked fear.

Boldin shot a look to left and right at his own men, dug in in the shallow holes at the edge of the slope. Their faces were an ashen green, eyes wide, wild and staring, their expressions no longer human. Even Teeth, the strong man of the Punishment Battalion, was poised there, eyes blank of everything save sheer unadulterated fear, dum-dum bullet held at an open breech, unable to insert it.

'Time to run?' Vulf whispered cunningly. 'Time…'

Boldin raised himself, his mouth open, as if he had suddenly made up his mind and were about to shout a command. In that very same moment the first of the crouched figures in that familiar coal-scuttle helmet came into sight. There was a great hush, as if some primeval monster had taken a huge breath and greedy flame shot out. A man screamed with unbearable agony as it wrapped itself around him, transforming him into a cruelly burning human torch instantly.

Number One Company broke immediately. Throwing away their weapons, screaming choking obscenities, limbs trembling uncontrollably, they streamed straight towards Katukov. Automatically he ripped off a burst. Men dropped twitching and writhing to the ground, while others swerved to left and right of the bullets, screaming deliriously, unafraid of that hammering fire, only concerned to escape the flaming horror to their rear.

Boldin rose to his feet. 'FIRE! ... FIRE, IN HEAVEN'S NAME — F-I-R-E!' he sobbed hysterically and raising a wildly trembling hand loosed off a crazy volley at the advancing Germans, yelling in hoarse triumph as they drove the fleeing Russians before them with their yellow-red roaring wall of fire.

Teeth screamed something, ignoring Tinleg vomiting at his feet. He thrust the dum-dum bullet into the breech, clicked home the bolt, sighted and fired.

The leading German stopped abruptly as if he had just run into a brick wall. His face disappeared in a crimson slurry. He slammed into his neighbour and brought him tumbling down too, the two of them clasped in each other's arms like passionate lovers. But the others still kept coming on, driving all before them with that terrible raging fire, burning everything, setting the very ground alight, turning their front into a roaring holocaust, in which the shadowy outlines of trapped men writhed and twisted in one last frantic dance until finally they were deposited on the smoking ground blackened skeletons, harsh claws raised as if in supplication.

The terrified survivors of the 1st Company swept through the last defenders. Nothing could stop them. Here and there an NCO sprang to his feet and held out his arms like a child trying to halt others in some kind of playground game. To no avail. Foam-flecked mouths wide open, uttering silent screams, eyes blank with unreasoning fear, they pelted on and past the NCOs, not even stopped by the bullets from their own comrades coming their way.

'Let them go,' Boldin, sweat streaming down his face, nostrils full of the stink of burning flesh, cried, 'let them go! Concentrate on the Fritzes!'

Furiously the men all around him in the line, knowing that their own lives depended upon it now, worked their bolts, firing, firing, throwing slug after slug and the advancing Germans with a speed they had never achieved before.

Here and there a German tumbled to the ground, but still they kept on advancing. Nothing could stop them now. Nothing! Boldin could feel that tremendous heat begin to scorch his face already. It was the end. In a minute his own men would break and make a run for it. The Gulag rats were finished at last.

'*Scheisse!*' Meier yelped as the slug whacked into his knee. He sat down suddenly and looked in a kind of bewilderment at the thin trickle of dark-red blood beginning to emerge from the ragged tear in his trousers just above his right knee like a timid animal coming from its lair. He had been shittingly well hit!

'*Hauptsturm…*' One of the men in the front rank dropped back and made as if he were about to bend and help him.

Irritably Meier waved his hand, still clutching his pistol, at the black-faced rifleman. 'Keep going,' he called above the screams of the fleeing Russians, 'see the Popovs off! I'll be all right... Keep going!'

Meier winced with pain. It wasn't bad, but it was bad enough. Just his luck to get shot when the Company had about routed the Popovs. Still, Papa Eicke would be proud of him. One single company of the *Totenkopf* had set a whole shitty Ivan battalion running! Even if the lace-panty gents of the *Wehrmacht* wouldn't recommend him for a piece of tin, Papa would. He touched his throat for a brief instant. Perhaps they might even cure his sore throat in Berlin for this business; it was worth it.

He dismissed that thought and, concentrating on his wound, dropped his pistol on the charred yellow grass next to him; he pulled the trench knife from his boot. With a quick slash, he ripped open the knee of his field-grey pants.

White flecks of bone showed through the ruddy gore of his kneecap. The sods had shot it to hell. That's why it didn't really hurt. All there was, was a kind of dull gnawing ache. *Shit*, he cursed to himself, forgetting his advancing men now, convinced that nothing could go wrong. Height 444 would be theirs in a matter of minutes. The bone-menders would probably have to patch it up with steel pins so that he'd be limping around on one stiff flipper for the rest of his days. Still, he told himself, it would have its advantages. He'd be a war hero, who had shed his blood for 'Folk, Fatherland and Führer', and had been awarded a decoration for bravery. The Party would take care of him. He'd be finished with the camps for good. Perhaps they'd make him *Kreisleiter*, a County Leader, in some nice provincial town where there'd be a bit of social life and the local ladies would not be disinclined to let them down for a handsome young war hero.

The thought cheered him and he busied himself with his knee, telling himself that his little war was over and he would come out of it safely, thank God! But there would be no Knight's Cross of the Iron Cross, no *Kreisleiter* position nor willing local ladies, who would let them down for a handsome young war hero, for *Haupsturmbannführer* Meier.

Just as he had finished clearing away the cloth from his shattered knee and had begun applying his fat field-dressing to the bleeding wound, his nostrils were suddenly assailed by that stink of garlic, human sweat and black tobacco that could only indicate the presence of a Russian nearby.

He swung round. The field-dressing fell from suddenly nerveless fingers. The hillside was abruptly swarming with squat figures in the wadded jackets of the Popovs' Far Eastern Army. '*Siberians!*' he cried.

There were hundreds, thousands, tens of thousands of them plodding up the slope from the canal, their faces impassive, inscrutable, revealing nothing, as if they might go on marching forward westwards like this until they reached Berlin itself.

In sudden fear, Meier tried to raise himself. He couldn't. His wounded knee gave beneath him with a sharp stab of pain. But Meier did not notice the pain; his fear was too great. They were coming straight towards him, clambering up the slope directly behind the creeping barrage which had now begun to give them cover!

Meier ducked. Shells howled down all around him, throwing up angry mushrooms of flying earth and red-hot steel. Earth pattered down on his bent head and he gasped as the blast dragged the very air from his lungs. Automatically he blinked his eyes. When he opened them the barrage had swept over him and was creeping further along the plateau and he was staring up at a bland, moonlike face.

Frantically the German sought for his pistol. It was gone. The Siberian followed the movement of his trembling anxious fingers, his face revealing nothing.

'*No … no…*' Meier screamed, knowing now the pistol wasn't there, 'I surrender… Do you hear, *I surrender!*' He raised his right hand, dripping with the blood from his wounded knee, to plead for mercy.

The Siberian's face showed no emotion. He raised the knife he was carrying in his other hand, opening his full-lipped mouth to show two gold molars. □

'Please —'

The Siberian's razor-sharp knife hissed. Meier screamed. A thin red line welled up along the whole length of his neck. The Siberian struck again, slashing savagely right and left, until his small hand was red with bloody gore to the wrist. Meier slumped forward, pink bubbles foaming at the edges of his gaping mouth.

Deliberately the Siberian wiped the blood off his knife on the dying German's tunic, then commenced to loot his body, while ahead of him the sledgehammer of the barrage struck home on the pits filled with mortally wounded Gulag rats and those who had buried themselves among the dead and dying to escape those terrible flame-throwers. But there was nothing to fear from them anymore, for they, too, were dead. And then the barrage was past, working its way down the far slope, deliberately, pedantically slaughtering everything in its path as it neared Manteuffel's HQ, where already the staff cars were being packed in panic and the white-faced, elegant officers toyed pointedly with their pistol holsters and looked hard at the trembling clerks running back and forth burning top secret documents, until finally the sickened little general gave that one-word command that freed them from all further responsibility and signalled the end of the German advance eastwards, for good: '*Los!*'

It was all over. The Germans would not come again.

EPILOGUE

'*Slava krasnaya armya*!' the weak Georgian voice called through the microphone and was echoed back and forth across the great square by the loudspeakers. *Long live the Red Army*!

'*Slava krasnaya armya*!' Ten thousand young voices called back the dictator's greeting without enthusiasm. Standing in the front rank of the newly reformed Punishment Battalion, Teeth, next to Tinleg, raised his leg slightly and gave one of his celebrated long insolent farts.

Katukov, his face still drawn and pale from his long weeks in the military hospital, where the bone-menders had removed what had been left of his right eye, now covered by a black patch, flushed. Boldin grinned. It was what he expected from his Gulag rats, veterans and new recruits from the camps alike. The yellow-faced dictator standing behind the bullet-proof glass partition on the balcony high above their heads, deserved nothing better. Not from *them*!

Then his face grew sombre as he remembered all those who had died. Livny, the one-armed Piotr, the handsome young lieutenant of Intelligence and a host of others. For what and for whom?

But before he could answer those overwhelming questions, Stalin began his little farewell speech to speed them on their way to the waiting trains which would carry them to the new front.

'Comrades, beloved soldiers, you have won the first battle of the Great Patriotic War. The Fascist enemy has been stopped before Moscow. He will not return.'

The dictator paused, as if he had expected applause and the young men below in the softly falling snowflakes could hear the deep rasp of his breathing over the microphone. 'But a new danger has arisen to our Fatherland. The Fascists are on the move again on the Volga, attempting to wrest that city which bears my own name from us.'

Boldin glanced at Katukov. The colonel nodded slightly. Now he, too, knew where they were bound for.

'But they will not take it. *Never!*' Stalin emphasized his point with a weak gesture of his clenched fist. 'We will hold it, just as we held our beloved Moscow.'

He paused again. But there was no reaction to his words. The young men standing in the ankle-deep soft snow had long spent all emotion. They were the shock troops, cannon-fodder to be thrown into the greedy bloody maw of the war machine once more and consumed.

'You my shock battalions will ensure that. Comrades, beloved soldiers, I salute you, the glorious Fatherland salutes you, the Russian people salutes you! *Slava krasnaya —*'

The traditional greeting ended in a thick rasping cough. But dutifully they roared back the words.

As if on a previously arranged signal, the Moscow Garrison Band struck up a lively march. Officers bellowed orders, their breath fogging grey on the icy air. Boldin caught one last glimpse of that yellow-faced monster who had ruined his life, all their lives, and then Katukov was yelling his commands and the battalion were swinging across Red Square, the noise of their boots muffled by the snow so that they seemed like an army of grey ghosts.

The Gulag rats were going to war again. Soon the Battle for Stalingrad would commence...

A NOTE TO THE READER

Dear Reader,

If you have enjoyed this novel enough to leave a review on **Amazon** and **Goodreads**, then we would be truly grateful.

Sapere Books

Sapere Books is an exciting new publisher of brilliant fiction and popular history.

To find out more about our latest releases and our monthly bargain books visit our website: **saperebooks.com**